Puffin Books
:or: Kaye Webb

The Duelling Machine

The time is the far-distant future and man has migrated from Earth at last. But in the Acquataine Cluster, one of the newly colonized galaxies outside the Milky Way, something has gone badly wrong. The Prime Minister has been challenged to a duel by the sinister Odal of the Kerak Worlds.

Their conflict must take place inside the famous Duelling Machine, a shared dream world where men can fight to the death without being physically hurt. Except that this time the Prime Minister emerges from the dream as good as dead. So it is up to Professor Leoh, the Machine's inventor, to avert further disaster. But how? – for the Machine now seems to have powers unknown to its own inventor. Perhaps it may even be used to bring the entire universe under the domination of a ruthless dictatorship.

This is an action-packed, fast-moving story, with an unusual climax, which can be funny and thought-provoking at the same time. Recommended to any reader over 10 who has ever wondered about the future of the universe.

Ben Bova

The Duelling Machine

Puffin Books
in association with Faber & Faber

This book was originally published in America, and American spelling has had to be retained in the text, though not on the cover, title page and half title.

Puffin Books
Penguin Books Ltd,
Harmondsworth, Middlesex, England
Penguin Books,
625 Madison Avenue, New York, New York 10022, U.S.A.
Penguin Books Australia Ltd,
Ringwood, Victoria, Australia
Penguin Books Canada Ltd,
2801 John Street, Markham, Ontario L3R 1B4, Canada
Penguin Books (N.Z.) Ltd,
182–190 Wairau Road, Auckland 10, New Zealand

First published in England by Faber & Faber Ltd 1971
Published in Puffin Books 1977

Copyright © Ben Bova, 1971

Made and printed in Great Britain by
C. Nicholls & Company Ltd
Set in Linotype Juliana

To Myron R. Lewis – Scholar, swordsman, friend
and inventor of the duelling machine

The Perfect Warrior

Dulaq rode the slide to the upper pedestrian level, stepped off, and walked over to the railing. The city stretched out all around him – broad avenues thronged with busy people, pedestrian walks, vehicle thoroughfares, air cars gliding between the gleaming, towering buildings.

And somewhere in this vast city was the man he must kill. The man who would kill him, perhaps.

It all seemed so real! The noise of the streets, the odors of the perfumed trees lining the walks, even the warmth of the reddish sun on his back as he scanned the scene before him.

It is an illusion, Dulaq reminded himself. *A clever, man-made hallucination. A figment of my own imagination amplified by a machine.*

But it seemed so very real.

Real or not, he had to find Odal before the sun set. Find him and kill him. Those were the terms of the duel. He fingered the stubby, cylindrical stat-wand in his tunic pocket. That was the weapon that he had chosen, his weapon, his own invention. And this was the environment he had picked: his city, busy, noisy, crowded. The metropolis Dulaq had known and loved since childhood.

Dulaq turned and glanced at the sun. It was halfway down toward the horizon. He had about three hours to find Odal. And when he did – kill or be killed.

Of course no one is actually hurt. That is the beauty of the machine. It allows one to settle a score, to work out aggressive feelings, without either mental or physical harm.

Dulaq shrugged. He was a roundish figure, moon-faced,

slightly stoop-shouldered. He had work to do. Unpleasant work for a civilized man, but the future of the Acquataine Cluster and the entire alliance of neighboring star systems could well depend on the outcome of this electronically synthesized dream.

He turned and walked down the elevated avenue, marveling at the sharp sensation of solidity that met each footstep on the paving. Children dashed by and rushed up to a toyshop window. Men of commerce strode along purposefully, but without missing a chance to eye the girls sauntering by.

I must have a marvelous imagination. Dulaq smiled to himself.

Then he thought of Odal, the blond, icy professional he was pitted against. Odal was an expert at all the weapons, a man of strength and cool precision, an emotionless tool in the hands of a ruthless politician. But how expert could he be with a stat-wand, when the first time he saw one was the moment before the duel began? And how well acquainted could he be with the metropolis, when he had spent most of his life in the military camps on the dreary planets of Kerak, sixty light-years from Acquatainia?

No, Odal would be helpless and lost in this situation. He would attempt to hide among the throngs of people. All Dulaq had to do was to find him.

The terms of the duel limited both men to the pedestrian walks of the commercial quarter of the city. Dulaq knew this area intimately, and he began a methodical search through the crowds for the tall, fair-haired, blue-eyed Odal.

And he saw him! After only a few minutes of walking down the major thoroughfare, he spotted his opponent, strolling calmly along a cross walk, at the level below. Dulaq hurried down the ramp, worked his way through the crowd, and saw the man again, tall and blond, unmistakable. Dulaq edged along behind him quietly, easily. No disturbance. No pushing. Plenty of time. They walked down the street for a quarter-hour while the distance between them slowly shrank from fifty meters to five.

Finally Dulaq was directly behind him, within arm's reach. He grasped the stat-wand and pulled it from his tunic. With one quick motion he touched it to the base of the man's skull and started to thumb the button that would release a killing bolt of energy.

The man turned suddenly. It wasn't Odal!

Dulaq jerked back in surprise. It couldn't be. He had seen his face. It was Odal ... and yet this man was a stranger. Dulaq felt the man's eyes on him as he turned and walked away quickly.

A *mistake*, he told himself. *You were overanxious. A good thing this is a hallucination, or the autopolice would be taking you in by now.*

And yet ... he had been so certain that it was Odal. A chill shuddered through him. He looked up, and there was his antagonist, on the thoroughfare above, at the precise spot where he himself had been a few minutes earlier. Their eyes met, and Odal's lips parted in a cold smile.

Dulaq hurried up the ramp. Odal was gone by the time he reached the upper level. *He couldn't have gotten far.*

Slowly, but very surely, Dulaq's hallucination crumbled into a nightmare. He'd spot Odal in the crowd, only to have him melt away. He'd find him again, but when he'd get closer, it would turn out to be another stranger. He felt the chill of the duelist's ice-blue eyes on him again and again, but when he turned there was no one there except the impersonal crowd.

Odal's face appeared again and again. Dulaq struggled through the throngs to find his opponent, only to have him vanish. The crowd seemed to be filled with tall blond men crisscrossing before Dulaq's dismayed eyes.

The shadows lengthened. The sun was setting. Dulaq could feel his heart pounding within him, and perspiration pouring from every square centimeter of his skin.

There he is! Yes, that is him. Definitely, positively him! Dulaq pushed through the homeward-bound crowds toward the figure of a tall blond man leaning casually against the safety railing of the city's main thoroughfare. It was Odal, the damned smiling confident Odal.

Dulaq pulled the wand from his tunic and battled across the surging crowd to the spot where Odal stood motionless, hands in pockets, watching him dispassionately. Dulaq came within arm's reach . . .

'TIME, GENTLEMEN. TIME IS UP. THE DUEL IS ENDED.'

The Acquataine Cluster was a rich jewel box of some three hundred stars, just outside the borders of the Terran Commonwealth. More than a thousand inhabited planets circled those stars. The capital planet – Acquatainia – held the Cluster's largest city. In this city was the Cluster's oldest university. And in the university stood the dueling machine.

High above the floor of the antiseptic-white chamber that housed the dueling machine was a narrow gallery. Before the machine had been installed, the chamber had been a lecture hall in the university. Now the rows of students' seats, the lecturer's dais and rostrum were gone. The room held only the machine, a grotesque collection of consoles, control desks, power units, association circuits, and the two booths where the duelists sat.

In the gallery – empty during ordinary duels – sat a privileged handful of newsmen.

'Time limit's up,' one of them said. 'Dulaq didn't get him.'

'Yeah, but he didn't get Dulaq either.'

The first one shrugged. 'Now he'll have to fight Odal on his terms.'

'Wait, they're coming out.'

Down on the floor below, Dulaq and his opponent emerged from their enclosed booths.

One of the newsmen whistled softly. 'Look at Dulaq's face ... it's positively gray.'

'I've never seen the Prime Minister so shaken.'

'And take a look at Kanus' hired assassin.' The newsmen turned toward Odal, who stood before his booth, quietly chatting with his seconds.

'Hmp. There's a bucket of frozen ammonia for you.'

'He's enjoying this.'

One of the newsmen stood up. 'I've got a deadline to meet. Save my seat.'

He made his way past the guarded door, down the ramp-way circling the outer wall of the building, to the portable tri-di camera unit that the Acquatainian government had permitted for the newsmen to make their reports.

The newsman huddled with his technicians for a few minutes, then stepped before the camera.

'Emile Dulaq, Prime Minister of the Acquataine Cluster and acknowledged leader of the coalition against Chancellor Kanus of the Kerak Worlds, has failed in the first part of his psychonic duel against Major Par Odal of Kerak. The two antagonists are now undergoing routine medical and psycho-logical checks before renewing their duel ...'

By the time the newsman returned to his gallery seat, the duel was almost ready to begin again.

Dulaq stood in the midst of his group of advisers before the looming impersonality of the machine. Across the way, Odal remained with his two seconds.

'You needn't go through with the next phase of the duel immediately,' one of the Prime Minister's advisers was say-ing. 'Wait until tomorrow. Rest and calm yourself.'

Dulaq's round face puckered into a frown. He cocked an eye at the chief meditech, hovering on the edge of the little group.

The meditech, one of the staff that ran the dueling machine, pointed out, 'The Prime Minister has passed the examina-tions. He is capable, within the rules of the duel, of resuming.'

'But he has the option of retiring for the day, doesn't he?'

'If Major Odal agrees.'

Dulaq shook his head impatiently. 'No. I shall go through with it. Now.'

'But . . .'

The Prime Minister's expression hardened. His advisers lapsed into a respectful silence. The chief meditech ushered Dulaq back into his booth. On the other side of the machine, Odal glanced at the Acquatainians, grinned humorlessly, and strode into his own booth.

Dulaq sat and tried to blank out his mind while the meditechs adjusted the neurocontacts to his head and torso. They finished and withdrew. He was alone in the booth now, looking at the dead-white walls, completely bare except for the large view screen before his eyes. The screen began to glow slightly, then brightened into a series of shifting colors. The colors merged and changed, swirling across his field of view. Dulaq felt himself being drawn into them, gradually, compellingly, completely immersed in them . . .

The mists slowly vanished and Dulaq found himself standing on an immense and totally barren plain. Not a tree, not a blade of grass; nothing but bare, rocky ground stretching in all directions to the horizon and a disturbingly harsh yellow sky. He looked down at his feet and saw the weapon that Odal had chosen. A primitive club.

With a sense of dread, Dulaq picked up the club and hefted it in his hand. He scanned the plain. Nothing. No hills or trees or bushes to hide in. No place to run to.

And off on the horizon he could see a tall, lithe figure holding a similar club walking slowly and deliberately toward him.

The press gallery was practically empty. The duel had more than an hour to run, and most of the newsmen were outside, broadcasting their hastily drawn guesses about Dulaq's failure to win with his own choice of weapons and environment.

Then a curious thing happened.

On the master control panel of the dueling machine, a single light flashed red. The chief meditech blinked at it in surprise, then pressed a series of buttons on his board. More red lights appeared. The chief meditech reached out and flipped a single switch.

One of the newsmen turned to his partner. 'What's going on down there?'

'I think it's all over . . . Yeah, look, they're opening up the booths. Somebody's scored a win.'

'But who?'

They watched intently while the other newsmen quickly filed back into the gallery.

'There's Odal. He looks happy.'

'Guess that means . . .'

'Good Lord! Look at Dulaq!'

*

More than two thousand light-years from Acquatainia was the star cluster called Carinae. Although it was an even greater distance away from Earth, Carinae was still well within the confines of the mammoth Terran Commonwealth. Dr Leoh, inventor of the dueling machine, was lecturing at the Carinae University when the news of Dulaq's duel reached him. An assistant professor perpetrated the unthinkable breach of interrupting the lecture to whisper the news in his ear.

Leoh nodded grimly, hurriedly finished his lecture, and then accompanied the assistant professor to the university president's office. They stood in silence as the slideway whisked them through the strolling students and blossoming greenery of the quietly busy campus.

Leoh was balding and jowly, the oldest man at the university. The oldest man anyone in the university knew, for that matter. But his face was creased from a smile that was almost habitual, and his eyes were active and alert. He wasn't smiling, though, as they left the slideway and entered the administration building.

They rode the lift tube to the president's office. Leoh asked the assistant professor as they stepped through the president's open doorway, 'You say he was in a state of catatonic shock when they removed him from the machine?'

'He still is,' the president answered from his desk. 'Completely withdrawn from the real world. Cannot speak, hear, or even see. A living vegetable.'

Leoh plopped down in the nearest chair and ran a hand across his fleshy face. 'I don't understand it. Nothing like this has ever happened in a dueling machine before.'

The president said, 'I don't understand it either. But, this is your business.' He put a slight emphasis on the last word, unconsciously perhaps.

'Well, at least this won't reflect on the university. That's why I formed Psychonics as a separate business enterprise.' Then Leoh grinned and added, 'The money, of course, was only a secondary consideration.'

The president managed a smile. 'Of course.'

'I suppose the Acquatainians want to talk to me?' Leoh asked academically.

'They're on tri-di now, waiting for you.'

'They're holding a transmission frequency open over two thousand light-years?' Leoh looked impressed.

'You're the inventor of the dueling machine and the head of Psychonics, Incorporated. You're the only man who can tell them what went wrong.'

'Well, I suppose I shouldn't keep them waiting.'

'You can take the call here,' the president said, starting to get up from his chair.

'No, no, stay at your desk,' Leoh insisted. 'There's no need for you to leave. Or you either,' he added to the assistant professor.

The president touched a button on his desk communicator.

The far wall of the office glowed momentarily, then seemed to dissolve. They were looking into another office, this one in distant Acquatainia. It was crowded with nervous-looking men in business clothes and military uniforms.

'Gentlemen,' Dr Leoh said.

Several of the Acquatainians tried to answer him at once. After a few seconds of talking simultaneously, they all looked toward one of their members – a tall, determined, shrewd-looking civilian who bore a neatly trimmed black beard.

'I am Fernd Massan, the Acting Prime Minister of Acquatainia. You realize, of course, the crisis that has been precipitated in my government because of this duel?'

Leoh blinked. 'I realize that there's apparently been some difficulty with one of the dueling machines installed in your cluster. Political crises are not in my field.'

'But your dueling machine had incapacitated the Prime Minister,' one of the generals bellowed.

'And at this particular moment,' a minister added, 'in the midst of our difficulties with the Kerak Worlds.'

Massan gestured them to silence.

'The dueling machine,' Leoh said calmly, 'is nothing more than a psychonic device ... it's no more dangerous than a tri-di communicator. It merely allows two men to share a dream world that they create together. They can do anything they want to in their dream world – settle an argument as violently as they wish, and neither of them is physically hurt any more than a normal dream can hurt you physically. Men can use the dueling machine as an outlet for their aggressive feelings, for their tensions and hatreds, without hurting themselves or their society.

'Your own government tested one of the machines and approved its use on Acquatainia more than three years ago. I see several of you who were among those to whom I personally demonstrated the machine. Dueling machines are becoming commonplace through wide portions of the Terran Commonwealth, and neighboring nations such as Acquatainia. I'm sure that many of you have used the machine yourselves. You have, General, I'm certain.'

The general flustered. 'That has nothing to do with the matter at hand!'

'Admittedly,' Leoh conceded. 'But I don't understand how a therapeutic machine can possibly become entangled in a political crisis.'

Massan said, 'Allow me to explain. Our government has been conducting extremely delicate negotiations with the governments of our neighboring star-nations. These negotiations concern the rearmament of the Kerak Worlds. You have heard of Kanus of Kerak?'

'Vaguely,' Leoh said. 'He's a political leader of some sort.'

'Of the worst sort. He has acquired complete dictatorship of the Kerak Worlds and is now attempting to rearm them for war. This is in direct contravention of the Treaty of Acquatainia, signed only thirty Terran years ago.'

'I see. The treaty was signed at the end of the Acquataine-Kerak War, wasn't it?'

'A war that we won,' the general pointed out.

'And now the Kerak Worlds want to rearm and try again,' Leoh said.

'Precisely.'

Leoh shrugged. 'Why not call in the Star Watch? This is their type of police activity. And what has all this to do with the dueling machine?'

'Let me explain,' Massan said patiently. He gestured to an aide, and on the wall behind him a huge tri-di star map glowed into life.

Leoh recognized it immediately: the swirling spiral of the Milky Way galaxy. From the rim of the galaxy, where the Sun and Earth were, in toward the star-rich heart of the Milky Way, stretched the Terran Commonwealth – thousands of stars and myriads of planets. On Massan's map the Commonwealth territory was shaded a delicate green. Just beyond its border was the golden cluster of Acquatainia.

Around it were names that Leoh knew only vaguely: Safad, Szarno, Etra, and a pinpoint marked Kerak.

'Neither the Acquataine Cluster nor our neighboring nations,' said Massan, 'have ever joined the Terran Commonwealth. Nor has Kerak, for that matter. Therefore the Star Watch can intervene only if all the nations concerned agree to intervention. Naturally Kanus would never accept the Star Watch. He *wants* to rearm.'

Leoh shook his head.

'As for the dueling machine,' Massan went on, 'Kanus has turned it into a political weapon ...'

'But that's impossible. Your government passed strict laws concerning the use of the machines. The dueling machine may be used only for personal grievances. It's strictly outside the realm of politics.'

Massan shook his head sadly. 'My dear Professor, laws are one thing, people are another. And politics consists of people, not words on tape.'

'I don't understand,' said Leoh.

'A little more than one Terran year ago, Kanus picked a quarrel with a neighboring nation – the Safad Federation. He wanted an especially favorable trade agreement with them. Their minister of trade objected most strenuously. One of the Kerak negotiators – a certain Major Odal – got into a personal argument with the minister. Before anyone knew what had happened, they had challenged each other to a duel. Odal won the duel, and the minister resigned his post. He said he could no longer fight against the will of Odal and Kerak ... he was psychologically incapable of it. Two weeks later he was dead – apparently a suicide, although I have my doubts.'

'That's ... extremely interesting,' Leoh said.

'Three days ago,' Massan continued, 'the same Major Odal engaged Prime Minister Dulaq in a bitter personal argument. Odal is now a military attaché of the Kerak embassy here on Acquatainia. The argument grew so loud before a large group at an embassy party that the prime minister had no alternative but to challenge Odal. And now . . .'

'And now Dulaq is in a state of shock, and your government is tottering.'

Massan's back stiffened. 'Our government will not fall, nor shall the Acquataine Cluster acquiesce to the rearmament of the Kerak Worlds. But . . .' his voice lowered, 'without Dulaq, our alliances with neighboring nations may dissolve. All our allies are smaller and weaker than Acquatainia. Kanus could pressure each one individually and make certain that they won't take steps to prevent his rearming Kerak. Alone, Acquatainia cannot stop Kanus.'

'But if Kerak attacks you, surely you could ask the Star Watch for help and . . .'

'It won't be that simple or clear-cut. Kanus will nibble off one small nation at a time. He can strike a blow and conquer a nation before the Star Watch can be summoned. Finally he'll have us cut off completely, without a single ally. Then he'll strike Acquatainia, or perhaps even try to subvert us from within. If he takes Acquatainia, he'll have whetted his appetite for bigger game: he'll want to conquer the Terran Commonwealth next. He'll stop at nothing.'

'And he's using the dueling machines to further his ambitions,' Leoh mused. 'Well, gentlemen, it seems I have no alternative but to travel to the Acquataine Cluster. The dueling machine is my responsibility, and if there's something wrong with it, or with the use of it, I'll do my best to correct the situation.'

'That is all we ask,' Massan said. 'Thank you.'

The Acquatainian scene faded away, and the three men in the president's office found themselves looking at a solid wall once again.

'Well,' Leoh said, turning to the president, 'it seems that I must request an indefinite leave of absence.'

The president frowned. 'And it seems that I must grant it – even though the year isn't even half-finished.'

'I regret the necessity,' said Leoh. Then, with a broad grin, he added, 'My assistant, here, can handle my courses for the remainder of the year quite easily. Perhaps he'll even be able to deliver his lectures without being interrupted.'

The assistant professor turned red from collar to scalp.

'Now then,' Leoh muttered to himself, 'who is this Kanus, and why is he trying to turn the Kerak Worlds into an arsenal?'

*

Chancellor Kanus, Supreme Leader of the Kerak Worlds, stood at the edge of the balcony and looked across the wild, tumbling gorge to the rugged mountains beyond.

'These are the forces that mold men's actions,' he said to his small audience of officials and advisers. 'The howling winds, the mighty mountains, the open sky, and the dark powers of the clouds.'

The men nodded and made murmurs of agreement.

'Just as the mountains thrust up from the pettiness of the lands below, so shall we rise above the common walk of men,' Kanus said. 'Just as a thunderstorm terrifies them, we will make them cower and bend to our will.'

'We will destroy the past,' said one of the ministers.

'And avenge the memory of defeat,' Kanus added. He turned and looked at the little group of men. Kanus was the smallest man on the balcony : short, spare, sallow-faced. His gaudy military uniform looked out of place on him, too big and heavy, too loaded with braid and medals. But he possessed piercing dark eyes and a strong voice that commanded attention.

He walked through the knot of men and stopped before a tall, lean, blond youth in a light-blue military uniform. 'And you, Major Odal, will be a primary instrument in the first steps of conquest.'

Odal bowed stiffly. 'I only hope to serve my Leader and my Worlds.'

'You shall. And you already have,' Kanus said, beaming.

'Already the Acquatainians are thrashing about like a snake whose head has been cut off. Without Dulaq, they have no brain to direct them. For your part in this triumph . . .' Kanus snapped his fingers, and one of his advisers quickly stepped to his side and handed him a small ebony box, 'I present you with this token of the esteem of the Kerak Worlds, and of my personal high regard.'

He handed the box to Odal, who opened it and took out a small jeweled pin.

'The Star of Kerak,' Kanus announced. 'This is the first time it has been awarded to anyone except a warrior on the battlefield. But, then, we have turned their so-called civilized dueling machine into our own battlefield, eh?'

Odal smiled. 'Yes, sir, we have. Thank you very much, sir. This is the supreme moment of my life.'

'To date, Major. Only to date. There will be other moments, even higher ones. Come inside. We have many plans to discuss . . . more duels . . . more triumphs.'

They all filed into Kanus' huge, elaborate office. The Leader walked across the plushly ornate room and sat at the elevated desk, while his followers arranged themselves on the chairs and couches placed about the floor. Odal remained standing, near the doorway.

Kanus let his fingers flick across a small control board set into his desk top, and a tri-dimensional star map appeared on the far wall. At its center were the eleven stars of the Kerak Worlds. Off to one side of the map was the Acquataine Cluster – wealthy, powerful, the most important political and economic power in this section of the galaxy. Farther away from Kerak, the slimmest edge of the Terran Commonwealth showed; to put the entire Commonwealth on the map would have dwarfed Acquatainia and made Kerak microscopic.

Pointing at the map, Kanus began one of his inevitable harangues. Objectives, political and military. Already the Kerak Worlds were unified under his dominant will. The people would follow wherever he led. Already the political alliances built up by Acquatainian diplomacy since the last war were tottering, now that Dulaq was out of the picture. Kerak was beginning to rearm. A political blow *here*, at the Szarno Confederacy, to bring them and their armaments industries into line with Kerak. Then a diplomatic alliance with the Etra Domain, which stood between the Acquataine Cluster and the Terran Commonwealth, to isolate the Acquatainians. Then, finally, the military blow against Acquatainia.

'A sudden strike, a quick, decisive series of blows, and the Acquatainians will collapse like a house of paper. Even if the Star Watch wanted to interfere, we would be victorious before they could bring help to the Acquataine Cluster. And with the resources of Acquatainia to draw on, we can challenge any force in the galaxy – even the Terran Commonwealth itself !'

The men in the room nodded and smiled.

They've heard this story many times, Odal thought. This was the first time he had been privileged to listen to it. If you closed your eyes, or looked only at the star map, the plan sounded bizarre, extreme, even impossible. But if you watched Kanus and let those piercing, almost hypnotic eyes fasten on yours, then the Leader's wildest dreams sounded not only exciting, but inevitable.

Odal leaned a shoulder against the paneled wall and looked at the other men in the room.

There was fat Greber, the Vice Chancellor, fighting desperately to stay awake after drinking too much wine during luncheon and afterward. And Modal, sitting on the couch next to him, was bright-eyed and alert, thinking only of how much money and power would come to him as Minister of Industry once the rearmament program went into full speed.

Sitting alone on another couch was Kor, the quiet one, the head of Intelligence and – technically – Odal's superior. Silent Kor, whose few words were usually charged with terror for those whom he spoke against. Kor had an unfathomed capacity for cruelty.

Marshal Lugal looked bored when Kanus spoke of politics, but his face changed when military matters came up. The Marshal lived for only one purpose: to avenge his army's humiliating defeat in the war against Acquatainia. What he didn't realize, Odal knew, was that as soon as he had reorganized the army and re-equipped it, Kanus planned to retire him and place younger men in charge. Men whose only loyalty was not to the army, nor even to the Kerak Worlds and their people, but to the Leader himself.

Eagerly following every syllable, every gesture of the Leader, was little Tinth. Born to the nobility, trained in the arts, a student of philosophy, Tinth had deserted his heritage to join the forces of Kanus. His reward was the Ministry of Education. Many teachers had suffered under him.

And finally there was Romis, the Minister of Foreign Affairs. A professional diplomat, one of the few men in government before Kanus' sweep to power who had survived this long. It was clear that Romis hated the Chancellor. But he served the Kerak Worlds well. The diplomatic corps was flawless in their handling of the Safad trade treaty, although they would have gotten nowhere without Odal's own work in the dueling machine. It was only a matter of time, Odal knew, before one of them – Romis or Kanus – killed the other.

The rest of Kanus' audience consisted of political hacks, roughnecks-turned-bodyguards, and a few other hangers-on who had been with Kanus since the days when he held his political monologues in cellars and haunted the alleys to avoid the police. Kanus had come a long way: from the blackness of oblivion to the dazzling heights of the Chancellor's rural estate.

Money, power, glory, revenge, patriotism: each man in the room, listening to Kanus, had his reason for following the Chancellor.

And my reasons? Odal asked himself. *Why do I follow? Can I see into my own mind as easily as I see into theirs?*

There was duty, of course. Odal was a soldier, and Kanus

was the duly elected Leader of the government. Once elected, though, he had dissolved the government and solidified his powers as absolute dictator of the Kerak Worlds.

There was gain to be had by performing well under Kanus. Regardless of his political ambitions and personal tyrannies, Kanus rewarded well when pleased. The medal – the Star of Kerak – carried with it an annual pension that would nicely accommodate a family. *If I had one,* Odal thought sardonically.

There was a power, of sorts, also. Working the dueling machine in his special way, hammering a man into nothingness, finding the weaknesses in his personality and exploiting them, pitting his mind against others, turning sneering towers of pride like Dulaq into helpless whipped dogs – that was power. And it was a power that did not go unnoticed in Kerak. Already Odal was easily recognized on the streets; girls especially seemed to be attracted to him now.

'The most important factor,' Kanus was saying, 'and I cannot stress it too heavily, is to build up an aura of invincibility. This is why your work is so important, Major Odal. You must be invincible! Because you represent the will of the Kerak Worlds. You are the instrument of my will, and you must triumph at every turn. The fate of your people and your Chancellor rests squarely on your shoulders each time you step into a dueling machine. You have borne that responsibility well, Major. Can you carry it even further?'

'I can, sir,' Odal answered crisply, 'and I will.'

Kanus beamed at him. 'Excellent! Because your next duel – and those that follow it – will be to the death.'

*

It took the star ship two weeks to make the journey from Carinae to the Acquataine Cluster. Dr Leoh spent the time checking over the Acquatainian dueling machine, by direct tri-di communication link. The Acquatainian government gave him all the technicians and time he needed for the task.

Leoh spent as much of his spare time as possible with the other passengers of the ship. They were all enormously wealthy, as star-ship travelers had to be, or else they were traveling on government business – and expense. He was gregarious, a fine conversationalist, and had a nicely balanced sense of humor. Particularly, he was a favorite of the younger women, since he had reached the age where he could flatter them with his attention without making them feel endangered. But still, there were long hours when he was alone in his stateroom with nothing but memories. At times like these, it was impossible not to think back over the road he had been following.

Albert Robertus Leoh, Ph.D., professor of physics, professor of electronics, master of computer technology, inventor of the interstellar tri-di communications system. And more recently, student of psychology, professor of psychophysiology, founder of Psychonics, Incorporated, inventor of the dueling machine.

During his youthful years, with enthusiasm unbridled by experience, Leoh had envisioned himself as helping mankind to spread its colonies and civilizations throughout the galaxy. The bitter century of galactic war had ended in his childhood, and now human societies were linked together across the stars into a more-or-less peaceful coalition of nations.

There were two great motivating forces at work on those human societies, and these forces worked toward opposite goals. On the one hand was the urge to explore, to reach new stars, new planets, to expand the frontiers of man's civilizations and found new colonies, new nations. Pitted against this drive to expand was an equally powerful force: the realization that technology had put an end to physical labor and almost to poverty itself on all the civilized worlds of man. The urge to move off to the frontier was penned in and buried alive under the enervating comforts of civilization.

The result was inescapable. The civilized worlds became

constantly more crowded. They became jam-packed islands of humanity sprinkled thinly across a sea of space that was still studded with unpopulated islands. The expense and difficulty of interstellar travel was often cited as an excuse. The star ships *were* expensive: their power demands were frightful. They could be used for business, for the pleasure of the very rich, for government travel; but hauling whole colonies of farmers and workers was almost completely out of the question. Only the most determined (and best financed) groups of colonists could afford them. The rest of mankind accepted the ease and safety of civilization, lived in the bulging cities of the teeming planets.

Their lives were circumscribed by their neighbors and by their governments. Constantly more people crowded into a fixed living space meant constantly less freedom. The freedom to dream, to run free, to procreate, all became state-owned, state-controlled privileges

And Leoh had contributed to this situation.

He had contributed his thoughts and his work. He had contributed often and regularly. The interstellar communications system was only one outstanding achievement in a long career of achievements.

Leoh had been nearly at the voluntary retirement age for scientists when he realized what he and his fellow scientists had done. Their efforts to make life richer and more rewarding had only made it less strenuous and more rigid. With every increase in physical comfort, Leoh discovered, came a corresponding increase in spiritual discomfort – in neuroses, in crimes of violence, in mental aberrations. Senseless wars of pride broke out between star-nations for the first time in generations. Outwardly, the peace of the galaxy was assured except for minor flare-ups; but beneath the glossy surface of man's civilization smoldered the beginnings of a volcano. Police actions fought by the Star Watch were increasing ominously. Petty wars between once-stable peoples were flaring up steadily.

Once Leoh realized the part he had played in all this, he was confronted with two emotions: a deep sense of guilt, both personal and professional; and, countering this, a determination to do something, anything, to restore at least some balance to man's collective mentality.

Leoh stepped out of physics and electronics, and entered the field of psychology. Instead of retiring, he applied for a beginner's status in his new profession. It took considerable bending and straining of the Commonwealth's rules, but for a man of Leoh's stature the rules could sometimes be flexed a little. Leoh became a student once again, then a researcher, and finally a professor of psychophysiology.

Out of this came the dueling machine. A combination of electroencephalograph and autocomputer. A dream machine that amplified a man's imagination until he could engulf himself in a world of his own making. Leoh envisioned it as a device to enable men to rid themselves of hostility and tension, safely. Certainly psychiatrists and psychotechnicians used the machines to treat their patients. But Leoh saw further, saw that – as a *dueling* machine – the psychonic device could be used to prevent mental tensions and disorders. And he convinced many governments to install dueling machines for that purpose.

When two men had a severe difference of opinion, deep enough to warrant legal action, they could go to the dueling machine instead of the courts. Instead of passively watching the machinations of the law grind impersonally through their differences, they could allow their imaginations free rein in the dueling machine. They could settle the argument as violently as they wished, without hurting themselves or anyone else. On most civilized worlds, the results of properly monitored duels were accepted as legally binding.

The tensions of civilized life could be escaped – temporarily – in the dueling machine. This was a powerful tool, much too powerful to allow it to be used indiscriminately. Therefore Leoh safeguarded his invention by forming a private company, Psychonics, Incorporated, and securing an exclusive license from the Terran Commonwealth to manufacture, sell, install, and maintain the machines. His customers were government health and legal agencies. His responsibilities were: legally, to the Commonwealth; morally, to all mankind; and finally to his own restless conscience.

The dueling machines succeeded. They worked as well, and often better, than Leoh had anticipated. But he knew that they were only a stopgap, only a temporary shoring of a constantly eroding dam. What was needed, really needed, was some method of exploding the status quo, some means of convincing people to reach out for those unoccupied, unexplored stars that filled the galaxy, some way of convincing men that they should leave the comforts of civilization for the excitement and freedom of new lands.

Leoh had been searching for that method when the news of Dulaq's duel had reached him. Now he was speeding across light-years of space, praying to himself that the dueling machine had not failed.

The two-week flight ended. The star ship took up a parking orbit around the capital planet of the Acquataine Cluster. The passengers trans-shipped to the surface.

Dr Leoh was met at the landing disk by an official delegation, headed by Massan, the Acting Prime Minister. They exchanged formal greetings at the base of the ship while the other passengers hurried by, curious, puzzled. As they rode the slideway toward a private entrance to the spaceport's administration building, Leoh commented:

'As you probably know, I have checked your dueling machine quite thoroughly via tri-di for the past two weeks. I can find nothing wrong with it.'

Massan shrugged. 'Perhaps you should have checked the machine on Szarno instead.'

'The Szarno Confederation? Their dueling machine?'

'Yes. This morning, Kanus' assassin killed a man in it.'

27

'He won another duel,' Leoh said.

'You do not understand,' Massan said grimly. 'Major Odal's opponent – an industrialist who had spoken out against Kanus – was actually killed in the dueling machine. The man is dead!'

*

One of the advantages of being Commander in Chief of the Star Watch, the old man thought to himself, is that you can visit any planet in the Commonwealth.

He stood at the top of the hill and looked out over the grassy tableland of Kenya. This was the land of his birth, Earth was his home world. The Star Watch's official headquarters was in the heart of a star cluster much closer to the center of the Commonwealth, but Earth was the place the Commander wanted most to see as he grew older and wearier.

An aide, who had been following the Commander at a respectful distance, suddenly intruded himself in the old man's reverie.

'Sir, a message for you.'

The Commander scowled at the young officer. 'Didn't I give express orders that I was not to be disturbed?'

The officer, slim and stiff in his black-and-silver uniform, replied, 'Your chief of staff passed the message on to you, sir. It's from Dr Leoh of Carinae University. Personal and urgent, sir.'

The old man grumbled to himself, but nodded. The aide placed a small crystalline sphere on the grass before the Commander. The air above the sphere started to vibrate and glow.

'Sir Harold Spencer here,' the Commander said.

The bubbling air seemed to draw in on itself and take solid form. Dr Leoh sat at a desk chair and looked up at the standing Commander.

'Harold, it's a pleasure to see you again,' Leoh said, getting up from the chair.

Spencer's stern eyes softened and his beefy face broke into a well-creased smile. 'Albert, you ancient sorcerer. What do you mean by interrupting my first visit home in fifteen years?'

'It won't be a long interruption,' Leoh said. 'I merely want to inform you of something . . .'

'You told my chief of staff that it was urgent,' Sir Harold groused.

'It is. But it's not the sort of problem that requires much action on your part. Yet. Are you familiar with recent political developments on the Kerak Worlds?'

Spencer snorted. 'I know that a barbarian named Kanus has taken over as dictator. He's a troublemaker. I've been trying to get the Commonwealth Council to let us quash him before he causes grief, but you know the Council . . . first wait until the flames have sprung up, then wail at the Star Watch to do something!'

Grinning, Leoh said, 'You're as irascible as ever.'

'My personality is not the subject of this rather expensive discussion. What about Kanus? And what are you doing, getting yourself involved in politics? About to change your profession again?'

'No, not at all,' Leoh answered with a laugh. Then, more seriously, 'It seems that Kanus has discovered a method of using the dueling machine to achieve political advantages over his neighbors.'

Leoh explained the circumstances of Odal's duels with Dulaq and the Szarno industrialist.

'Dulaq is completely incapacitated and the other poor fellow is dead?' Spencer's face darkened into a thundercloud. 'You were right to call me. This is a situation that could quickly become intolerable.'

'I agree,' said Leoh. 'But evidently Kanus hasn't broken any laws or interstellar agreements. All that meets the eye is a disturbing pair of accidents, both of them accruing to Kanus' benefit.'

'Do you believe they were accidents?'

'Certainly not. The dueling machine can't cause physical

or mental harm ... unless someone's tampered with it in some way.'

Spencer was silent for a moment, weighing the matter in his mind. 'Very well. The Star Watch cannot act officially but there's nothing to prevent me from dispatching an officer to the Acquataine Cluster on detached duty, to serve as liaison between us.'

'Good. I think that will be the most effective way of handling the situation, at present.'

'It will be done.'

Sir Harold's aide made a mental note of it.

'Thanks very much,' Leoh said. 'Now go back to enjoying your vacation.'

'Vacation? This is no vacation. I happen to be celebrating my birthday.'

'So? Well, congratulations. I try not to remember mine,' said Leoh.

'Then you must be older than I,' Spencer replied, allowing only the faintest hint of a smile to appear.

'I suppose it's possible.'

'But not very likely, eh?'

They laughed together and said good-by. The Star Watch Commander tramped through the grassland until sunset, enjoying the sight of the greenery and the distant purple mountains he had known from childhood. As dusk closed in, he told the aide he was ready to leave.

The aide pressed a stud on his belt and a two-place air car skimmed silently from the far side of the hills and hovered beside them. Spencer climbed in laboriously while the aide stayed discreetly at his side. As the Commander settled his bulk into his seat the aide hurried around the car and hopped into his place. The car glided off toward Spencer's planet ship, waiting for him at a nearby field.

'Don't forget to assign an officer to Dr Leoh,' Spencer muttered to his aide. Then he turned to watch the unmatchable beauty of an Earthly sunset.

The aide did not forget the assignment. That night, as Sir Harold's ship spiraled out to a rendezvous with a star ship, the aide dictated the necessary order to an autodispatcher that immediately beamed it to the Star Watch's nearest communications center, on Mars.

The order was scanned and routed automatically and finally beamed to the Star Watch unit commandant in charge of the area closest to the Acquataine Cluster, on the sixth planet circling the star Perseus Alpha. Here again the order was processed automatically and routed through the local headquarters to the personnel files. The automated files selected three microcard dossiers that matched the requirements of the order.

The three microcards and the order itself appeared simultaneously on the desk-top viewer of the Star Watch personnel officer at Perseus Alpha VI. He looked at the order, then read the dossiers. He flicked a button that gave him an updated status report on each of the three men in question. One was due for leave after an extended period of duty. The second was the son of a personal friend of the local commandant. The third had just arrived a few weeks ago, fresh from the Star Watch Academy.

The personnel officer selected the third man, routed his dossier and Sir Harold's order back into the automatic processing system, and returned to the film of primitive dancing girls that he had been watching before this matter of decision had arrived at his desk.

*

The space station that orbited Acquatainia's capital planet served simultaneously as a transfer point from star ships to planet ship, a tourist resort, meteorological station, scientific laboratory, communications center, astronomical observatory, medical haven for allergy and cardiac patients, and military base. It was, in reality, a good-sized city with its own markets, government, and a way of life.

Dr Leoh had just stepped off the debarking ramp of the

star ship from Szarno. The trip there had been pointless and fruitless. But he had gone anyway, in the slim hope that he might find something wrong with the dueling machine that had been used to murder a man. A shudder went through him as he edged through the automated customs scanners and identification checkers. What kind of people could these men of Kerak be? To actually kill a human being deliberately. To purposely plan the death of a fellow man. Worse than barbaric. Savage.

He felt tired as he left customs and took the slideway to the planetary shuttle ships. Even the civilized hubbub of travelers and tourists was bothering him, despite the sound-deadening plastics of the slideway corridor. He decided to check at the communications desk for messages. That Star Watch officer that Sir Harold had promised him a week ago should have arrived by now.

The communications desk consisted of a small booth that contained the output printer of a computer and an attractive dark-haired girl. Automation or not, Leoh decided, no machine can replace a girl's smile.

A lanky, thin-faced youth was half-leaning on the booth's counter, his legs crossed nervously. He was trying to talk to the girl. He had curly blond hair and crystal blue eyes; his clothes consisted of an ill-fitting pair of slacks and a tunic. A small traveler's kit rested on the floor by his feet.

'So, I was sort of, well, thinking ... maybe somebody might, uh, show me around ... a little,' he was stammering to the girl. 'I've never been, uh here ... I mean on Acquatainia, that is ... before ...'

'It's the most beautiful planet in the galaxy,' said the girl. 'Its cities are the finest.'

'Yes ... well, I was sort of thinking ... that is, maybe you ... eh ...'

She smiled coolly. 'I very seldom leave the station. There's so much to see and do here.'

'Oh ...'

'You're making a mistake,' Leoh interrupted. 'If you have such a beautiful planet for your home world, why in the name of the gods of intellect don't you go down there and enjoy it? I'll wager you haven't been out in the natural beauty and fine cities you spoke of since you started working here at the station.'

'Why, you're right,' she said, surprised.

'You see? You youngsters are all alike. You never think further than the ends of your noses. You should return to the planet, young lady, and see the sunshine again. Why don't you visit the university at the capital city? Plenty of open space and greenery, lots of sunshine and available young men!'

Leoh was grinning broadly and the girl smiled back at him. 'Perhaps I will,' she said.

'Ask for me when you get to the university. I'm Dr Leoh. I'll see to it that you're introduced to some of the students.'

'Why ... thank you, Doctor. I'll do it this week-end.'

'Good. Now then, any messages for me? Anyone aboard the station looking for me?'

The girl turned and tapped a few keys on the computer's control desk. A row of lights flicked briefly across the console's face. She turned back to Leoh:

'No, sir, I'm sorry. Nothing.'

'Hmp. That's strange. Well, thank you ... And I'll expect to see you this week-end.'

The girl smiled a farewell. Leoh started to walk away from the booth, back toward the slideway. The young man took a step toward him, stumbled on his own travel kit, and staggered across the floor for a half-dozen steps before regaining his balance. Leoh turned and saw that the youth's face bore a somewhat ridiculous expression of mixed indecision and curiosity.

'Can I help you?' Leoh asked, stopping at the edge of the slideway.

'How ... how did you do that, sir?'

'Do what?'

'Get that girl to agree to visit the university. I've been well, sort of talking to her for half an hour and she ... uh, she wouldn't even look straight at me.'

Leoh broke into a chuckle. 'Well, young man, to begin with, you were much too flustered. It made you appear over-anxious. On the other hand, I'm at an age where I can be fatherly. She was on guard against you, but not against me.'

'I see ... I think.'

'Yes.' Leoh gestured toward the slideway. 'I suppose this is where we go our separate ways.'

'Oh no, sir. I'm going with you. That is, I mean ... you *are* Dr Leoh, aren't you?'

'Yes, I am. And you must be ...' Leoh hesitated. *Can this be a Star Watch Officer?* he wondered.

The youth stiffened to attention and for an absurd flash of a second Leoh thought he was going to salute. 'Junior Lieutenant Hector, sir; on special detached duty from cruiser SW4–J188, home base Perseus Alpha VI.'

'I see,' Leoh replied. 'Hmm ... Is Hector your first name or your last?'

'Both, sir.'

I should have guessed, Leoh told himself. Aloud, he said, 'All right, Lieutenant, we'd better get to the shuttle before it leaves without us.'

They took to the slideway. Half a second later, Hector jumped off and dashed back to the communications booth for his travel kit. He hurried back to Leoh, bumping into seven bewildered citizens of various descriptions and nearly breaking both his legs when he tripped as he ran back onto the moving slideway. He went down on his face, sprawled across two lanes moving at different speeds and needed the assistance of an elderly lady before he was again on his feet and standing beside Leoh.

'I ... I'm sorry to cause all that, uh, commotion, sir.'

'That's all right. You weren't hurt, were you?'

'Uh, no ... I don't think so. Just embarrassed.'

Leoh said nothing. They rode the slideway in silence through the busy station and out to the enclosed berths where the planetary shuttles were docked. They boarded one of the ships and found a pair of seats.

'Just how long have you been with the Star Watch, Lieutenant?'

'Six weeks, sir. Three weeks aboard a star ship bringing me out to Perseus Alpha VI, a week at the planetary base there, and two weeks aboard the cruiser . . . um, SW4–J188, that is. The crew called her *Old Lardbucket* . . . after the captain, I think. Oh, I mean, six weeks since I received my commission. . . . I've been at the, uh, academy for four years.'

'You got through the academy in four years?'

'That's the regulation time, sir.'

'Yes, I know.'

The ship eased out of its berth. There was a moment of free fall, then the drive engine came on and weight returned to the passenger cabin.

'Tell me, Lieutenant, how did you get picked for this assignment?'

'I wish I knew, sir,' Hector said, his lean face wrinkling into a puzzled frown. 'I was working out a program for the navigation officer . . . aboard the cruiser. I'm pretty good at that . . . I can work out computer programs in my head, pretty much. Mathematics was my best subject at the academy.'

'Interesting.'

'Yes, well, anyway, I was working out this program when the captain himself came on deck and started shaking my hand and telling me that I was being sent on special duty at Acquatainia by direct orders of the Commander in Chief. He seemed very happy . . . the captain, that is.'

'He was probably pleased to see you get such an unusual assignment,' said Leoh, tactfully.

'I'm not so sure,' Hector answered truthfully. 'I think he regarded me as . . . well, some sort of a, um, problem. He had me on a different duty berth practically every day I was aboard the ship.'

'Well now,' Leoh changed the subject, 'what do you know about psychonics?'

'About what, sir?'

'Er . . . electroencephalography?'

Hector looked blank.

'Psychology, perhaps?' Leoh suggested hopefully. 'Physiology? Computer molectronics?'

'I'm pretty good at mathematics!'

'Yes, I know. Did you, by any chance, receive any training in diplomatic affairs?'

'At the Star Watch Academy? No, sir.'

Leoh ran a hand through his thinning hair. 'Then why did the Star Watch select you for this job? I must confess, Lieutenant, that I can't understand the workings of a military organization.'

Hector shook his head ruefully. 'Neither do I, sir.'

*

The next week was an enervatingly slow one for Leoh, evenly divided between a tedious checking of each component of the dueling machine, and shameless ruses to keep Hector as far away from the machine as possible.

The Star Watchman certainly wanted to help, and he actually was little short of brilliant in handling intricate mathematics completely in his head. But he was also, Leoh found, a clumsy, chattering, whistling, scatter-brained, inexperienced bundle of noise and nerves. It was impossible to do constructive work with him nearby.

Perhaps you're judging him too harshly, Leoh warned himself. *You might be letting your frustrations with the machine get the better of your sense of balance.*

The professor was sitting in the office that the Acquatainians had given him in one end of the former lecture hall that now held the dueling machine. Leoh could see its impassive metal hulk through the open office door. The room he was sitting in had been one of a suite of offices used by the permanent staff of the machine. But they had moved out of the building completely, in deference (or was it jealousy) to Leoh, and the Acquatainian government had turned the cubbyhole offices into living quarters for Leoh and the Star Watchman.

Leoh slouched back in his desk chair and cast a weary eye on the stack of papers that recorded the latest performance of the machine. Earlier that day he had taken the electro-encephalographic records of clinical cases of catatonia and run them through the machine's input circuits. The machine immediately rejected them, refused to process them through the amplification units and association circuits. In other words, the machine had recognized the EEG traces as something harmful to human beings.

Then how did it happen to Dulaq? Leoh asked himself for the thousandth time. It couldn't have been the machine's fault; it must have been something in Odal's mind that overpowered Dulaq's.

'Overpowered?' That's a terribly unscientific term, Leoh argued against himself.

Before he could carry the debate any further, he heard the main door of the big chamber slide open and bang shut, and Hector's off-key whistle shrilled and echoed through the high-vaulted room.

Leoh sighed and put his self-contained argument off to the back of his mind. Trying to think logically near Hector was a hopeless prospect.

'Are you in, Professor?' the Star Watchman's voice rang out.

'In here.'

Hector ducked in through the doorway and plopped his rangy frame on the couch.

'Everything going well, sir?'

Leoh shrugged. 'Not very well, I'm afraid. I can't find anything wrong with the dueling machine. I can't even *force* it to malfunction.'

'Well, that's good, isn't it?' Hector chirped happily.

'In a sense,' Leoh admitted, feeling slightly nettled at the youth's boundless, pointless optimism. 'But, you see, it means that Kanus' people can do things with the machine that I can't.'

Hector considered the problem. 'Hmm ... yes, I guess that's right too, isn't it?'

'Did you see the girl back to her ship safely?' Leoh asked.

'Yessir,' Hector replied, bobbing his head vigorously. 'She's on her way back to the communications booth at the space station. She said to tell you thanks and she enjoyed the visit a lot.'

'Good. It was very good of you to escort her around the campus. It kept her out of my hair ... what's left of it, that is.'

Hector grinned. 'Oh, I liked taking her around and all that ... and, well, it sort of kept *me* out of your hair too, didn't it?'

Leoh's eyebrows shot up in surprise.

Laughing, Hector said, 'Professor, I may be clumsy, and I'm sure no scientist ... but I'm not completely brainless.'

'I'm sorry if I gave you that impression.'

'Oh no ... don't be sorry. I didn't mean that to sound ... well, the way it sounded ... That is, I know I'm just in your way ...' He started to get up.

Leoh waved him back to the couch. 'Relax, my boy, relax. You know, I've been sitting here all afternoon wondering what to do next. Somehow, just now, I've come to a conclusion.'

'Yes?'

'I'm going to leave the Acquataine Cluster and return to Carinae.'

'What? But you can't! I mean ...'

'Why not? I'm not accomplishing anything here. Whatever it is that this Odal and Kanus have been doing, it's basically a political problem, not a scientific one. The professional staff of the machine here will catch up to their tricks, sooner or later.'

'But sir, if you can't find the answer, how can they?'

'Frankly, I don't know. But, as I said, this is a political problem more than a scientific one. I'm tired and frustrated and I'm feeling my years. I want to return to Carinae and spend the next few months considering beautifully abstract problems such as instantaneous transportation devices. Let Massan and the Star Watch worry about Kanus.'

'Oh! That's what I came to tell you. Massan has been challenged to a duel by Odal.'

'What?'

'This afternoon. Odal went to the Capital building and picked an argument with Massan right in the main corridor and challenged him.'

'Massan accepted?' Leoh asked.

Hector nodded.

Leoh leaned across his desk and reached for the phone. It took a few minutes and a few levels of secretaries and assistants, but finally Massan's dark, bearded face appeared on the screen above the desk.

'You've accepted Odal's challenge?' Leoh asked, without preliminaries.

'We meet next week,' Massan replied gravely.

'You should have refused.'

'On what pretext?'

'No pretext. A flat refusal, based on the certainty that Odal or someone else from Kerak is tampering with the dueling machine.'

Massan shook his head sadly. 'My dear learned sir, you do not comprehend the political situation. The government of Acquatainia is much closer to dissolution than I dare to admit publicly. The coalition of star-nations that Dulaq had constructed to keep Kerak neutralized has spoken apart

39

completely. Kerak is already arming. This morning, Kanus announced he would annex Szarno, with its enormous armaments industry. This afternoon, Odal challenges me.'

'I think I see . . .'

'Of course. The Acquataine government is paralyzed now, until the outcome of the duel is known. We cannot effectively intervene in the Szarno crisis until we know who will be heading the government next week. And, frankly, more than a few members of the Cabinet are now openly favoring Kanus and arguing that we should establish friendly relations with him before it is too late.'

'But that's all the more reason for refusing the duel,' Leoh insisted.

'And be accused of cowardice in my own Cabinet meetings?' Massan shook his head. 'In politics, my dear sir, the *appearance* of a man means much – sometimes more than his substance. As a coward, I would soon be out of office. But, perhaps, as the winner of a duel against the invincible Odal . . . or even as a martyr . . . I may accomplish something useful.'

Leoh said nothing.

Massan continued, 'I put off the duel for a week, which is the longest time I dare to postpone. I hope that in that time you can discover Odal's secret. As it is, the political situation may collapse about our heads at any moment.'

'I'll take the machine apart and rebuild it again, molecule by molecule,' Leoh promised.

As Massan's image faded from the screen, Leoh turned to Hector. 'We have one week to save his life.'

'And, uh, maybe prevent a war,' Hector added.

'Yes.' Leoh leaned back in his chair and stared off into infinity.

Hector shuffled his feet, rubbed his nose, whistled a few bars of off-key tunes, and finally blurted, 'How can you take apart the dueling machine?'

'Hmm?' Leoh snapped out of his reverie.

'How can you take apart the dueling machine?' Hector repeated. 'I mean ... well, it's a big job to do in a week.'

'Yes, it is. But, my boy, perhaps we – the two of us – can do it.'

Hector scratched his head. 'Well, uh, sir ... I'm not very ... that is, my mechanical aptitude scores at the academy ...'

Leoh smiled at him. 'No need for mechanical aptitude, my boy. You were trained to fight, weren't you? We can do this job mentally.'

*

It was the strangest week of their lives.

Leoh's plan was straightforward : to test the dueling machine, push it to the limits of its performance, by actually operating it – by fighting duels.

They started off easily enough, tentatively probing and flexing their mental muscles. Leoh had used the machines himself many times in the past, but only in tests of the system's routine performance. Never in actual combat against another human being. To Hector, of course, the machine was a totally new and different experience.

The Acquatainian staff plunged into the project without question, providing Leoh with invaluable help in monitoring and analyzing the duels.

At first, Leoh and Hector did nothing more than play hide-and-seek, with one of them picking an environment and the other trying to find him. They wandered through jungles and cities, over glaciers and interplanetary voids, all without ever leaving the dueling machine booths.

Then, when Leoh was satisfied that the machine could reproduce and amplify thought patterns with strict fidelity, they began to fight light duels. They fenced with blunted foils. Leoh did poorly, because he knew nothing about fencing, and his reflexes were much slower than Hector's. The dueling machine did not change a man's knowledge or his physical abilities; it only projected them into a dream he was sharing with another man. It matched Leoh's skills and

41

knowledge against Hector's. Then they tried other weapons – pistols, sonic beams, grenades – but always with the precaution of imagining themselves to be wearing protective equipment. Strangely, even though Hector was trained in the use of these weapons, Leoh won almost all the bouts. He was neither faster nor more accurate when they were target-shooting. But when the two of them faced each other, somehow Leoh almost always won.

The machine projects more than thoughts, Leoh began to realize. *It projects personality.*

They worked in the dueling machine day and night now, enclosed in the booths for twelve or more hours a day, driving themselves and the machine's regular staff to near exhaustion. When they gulped their meals, between duels, they were physically ragged and sharp-tempered. They usually fell asleep in Leoh's office, discussing the results of the day's work.

The duels slowly grew more serious. Leoh was pushing the machine to its limits now, carefully extending the rigors of each bout. Even though he knew exactly what and how much he intended to do in each fight, it often took a conscious effort to remind himself that the battles he was fighting were actually imaginary.

As the duels became more dangerous, and the artificially amplified hallucinations began to end in blood and death, Leoh found himself winning more and more frequently. With one part of his mind he was driving to analyze the cause of his consistent success. But another part of him was beginning to enjoy his prowess.

The strain was telling on Hector. The physical exertion of constant work and practically no relief was considerable in itself. But the emotional effects of being 'hurt' and 'killed' repeatedly were infinitely worse.

'Perhaps we should stop for a while,' Leoh suggested after the fourth day of tests.

'No, I'm all right.'

Leoh looked at him. Hector's face was haggard, his eyes bleary.

'You've had enough,' Leoh said quietly.

'Please don't make me stop,' Hector begged. 'I ... I can't stop now. Please give me a chance to do better. I'm improving ... I lasted twice as long in this afternoon's duels as I did this morning. Please, don't end it now ... not while I'm completely lost ...'

Leoh stared at him. 'You want to go on?'

'Yes, sir.'

'And if I say no?'

Hector hesitated. Leoh sensed he was struggling with himself. 'If you say no,' he answered dully, 'then it'll be no. I can't argue against you any more.'

Leoh was silent for a long moment. Finally he opened a desk drawer and took a small bottle from it. 'Here, take a sleep capsule. When you wake up we'll try again.'

It was dawn when they began again. Leoh entered the dueling machine determined to let Hector win. He gave the youthful Star Watchman his choice of weapons and environment. Hector picked one-man scout ships in planetary orbits. Their weapons were conventional laser beams.

But despite his own conscious desire, Leoh found himself winning! The ships spiraled around an unnamed planet, their paths intersecting at least once in every orbit. The problem was to estimate your opponent's orbital position, and then program your own ship so that you would arrive at that position either behind or to one side of him. Then you could train your guns on him before he could turn on you.

The problem should have been an easy one for Hector, with his knack for intuitive mental calculation. But Leoh scored the first hit. Hector had piloted his ship into an excellent firing position, but his shot went wide. Leoh maneuvered clumsily, but he managed to register a trifling hit on the side of Hector's ship.

In the next three passes, Leoh scored two more hits.

Hector's ship was badly damaged now. In return, the Star Watchman had landed one glancing shot on Leoh's ship. They came around again, and once more Leoh had outguessed his young opponent. He trained his guns on Hector's ship, then hesitated with his hand poised above the firing button.

Don't kill him again, he warned himself. *His mind can't take another defeat.*

But Leoh's hand, almost of its own will, reached the button and touched it lightly; another gram of pressure and the guns would fire.

In that instant's hesitation, Hector pulled his crippled ship around and aimed at Leoh. The Watchman fired a searing blast that jarred Leoh's ship from end to end. Leoh's hand slammed down on the firing button; whether he intended to do it or not, he didn't know.

Leoh's shot raked Hector's ship but didn't stop it. The two vehicles were hurtling directly at each other. Leoh tried desperately to avert a collision, but Hector bore in grimly, matching Leoh's maneuvers with his own.

The two ships smashed together and exploded.

Abruptly, Leoh found himself in the cramped booth of the dueling machine, his body cold and damp with perspiration, his hands trembling.

He squeezed out of the booth and took a deep breath. Warm sunlight was streaming into the high-vaulted room. The white walls gleamed brilliantly. Through the tall windows he could see trees and early students and clouds in the sky.

Hector walked up to him. For the first time in several days, the Watchman was smiling. Not much, but smiling. 'Well, we . . . uh, broke even on that one.'

Leoh smiled back, somewhat shakily. 'Yes. It was . . . quite an experience. I've never died before.'

Hector fidgeted. 'It's not so bad, I guess. It . . . sort of, well, it sort of shatters you, though.'

'Yes. I can see that now.'

'Try another duel?' Hector asked, nodding toward the machine.

'No. Not now. Let's get out of this place for a few hours. Are you hungry?'

'Starved.'

They fought several more duels over the next day and a half. Hector won three of them. It was late afternoon when Leoh called a halt.

'We can get in another couple,' the Watchman said.

'No need,' said Leoh. 'I have all the data I require. Tomorrow Massan meets Odal, unless we can put a stop to it. We've got much to do before tomorrow morning.'

Hector sagged into the couch. 'Just as well. I think I've aged seven years in the past seven days.'

'No, my boy,' Leoh said gently, 'you haven't aged. You've matured.'

*

It was deep twilight when the ground car slid to a halt on its cushion of compressed air before the Kerak embassy.

'I still think it's a mistake to go in there,' Hector said. 'I mean, you could've called him on the tri-di, couldn't you?'

Leoh shook his head. 'Never give an agency of any government the opportunity to say, "hold the line a moment." They huddle together and consider what to do with you. Nineteen times out of twenty, they'll end by passing you to another department or transferring your call to a taped, "So sorry," message.'

'Still,' Hector insisted, 'you're sort of, well, stepping into enemy territory.'

'They wouldn't dare harm us.'

Hector didn't reply, but he looked unconvinced.

'Look,' Leoh said, 'there are only two men alive who can shed light on this matter. One of them is Dulaq, and his mind is closed to us for an indefinite time. Odal is the only other man who knows what happened in those duels.'

Hector shook his head skeptically. Leoh shrugged, and

opened the door of the ground car. Hector had no choice but to get out and follow him as he walked up the pathway to the main entrance of the embassy building. The building stood gaunt and gray in the dusk, surrounded by a precisely clipped hedge. The entrance was flanked by a pair of evergreen trees, straight and spare as sentries.

Leoh and Hector were met just inside the entrance by a female receptionist. She looked just a trifle disheveled, as though she'd been rushed to her desk at a moment's notice. They asked for Odal, were ushered into a sitting-room, and within a few minutes – to Hector's surprise – were informed by the girl that Major Odal would be with them shortly.

'You see,' Leoh pointed out jovially, 'when you come in person they haven't as much of a chance to consider how to get rid of you.'

Hector glanced around the windowless room and contemplated the thick, solidly closed door. 'There's a lot of scurrying going on behind that door, I'll bet. I mean ... they might be figuring out how to get rid of us ... uh, permanently.'

Leoh was about to reply when the door opened and Odal came into the room. He wore a military uniform of light blue, with his insignia of rank on the shoulders and the Star of Kerak on his breast.

'Dr Leoh, I'm flattered,' he said with a slight bow. 'And Mr Hector ... or is it Lieutenant Hector?'

'Junior Lieutenant Hector,' the Watchman answered, with a curtness that surprised Leoh.

'Lieutenant Hector is assisting me,' the Professor said, 'and acting as liaison for Commander Spencer.'

'So,' Odal commented. He gestured them to be seated. Hector and Leoh placed themselves on a plush couch while Odal drew up a stiff chair, facing them. 'Now, why have you come to see me?'

'I want you to postpone your duel against Minister Massan tomorrow,' Leoh said.

Odal's lean face broke into a tight smile. 'Has Massan agreed to a postponement?'

'No.'

'Then why should I?'

'To be perfectly frank, Major, I suspect that someone is tampering with the machine used in your duels. For the moment, let's say that you have no knowledge of this. I am asking you to forego any further duels until we get to the bottom of this. The dueling machines are not to be used for political assassinations.'

Odal's smile faded. 'I regret, Professor, that I cannot postpone the duel. As for tampering with the machines, I can assure you that neither I nor anyone of the Kerak Worlds has touched the machines in any unauthorized manner.'

'Perhaps you don't fully understand the situation,' Leoh said. 'In the past week we've tested the dueling machine here on Acquatainia exhaustively. We've learned that its performance can be greatly influenced by a man's personality and his attitude. You've fought many duels in the machines. Your background of experience, both as a professional soldier and in the machines, gives you a decided advantage over your opponents.

'However, even with all this considered, I'm still convinced that no one can kill a man in the machine – under normal circumstances. We've demonstrated that fact in our tests. An unsabotaged machine cannot cause actual physical harm.

'Yet you've already killed one man and incapacitated another. Where will it stop?'

Odal's face remained calm, except for the faintest glitter of fire deep in his eyes. His voice was quiet, but it had the edge of a well-honed blade to it. 'I cannot be blamed for my background and experience. And I have not tampered with your machine.'

The door to the room opened, and a short, thickset, bullet-headed man entered. He was dressed in a dark street suit, so that it was impossible to guess his station at the embassy.

'Would the gentlemen care for some refreshments?' he asked in a low-pitched voice.

'No thank you,' Leoh said.

'Some Kerak wine, perhaps?'

'Well . . .'

'I, uh, don't think we'd better, sir,' Hector said. 'Thanks all the same.'

The man shrugged and sat at a chair next to the door.

Odal turned back to Leoh. 'Sir, I have my duty. Massan and I duel tomorrow. There is no possibility of postponing it.'

'Very well,' Leoh said. 'Will you at least allow me to place some special instrumentation into the booth with you, so that we can monitor the duel more fully? We can do the same thing with Massan. I know that duels are normally private and you'd be within your legal rights to refuse the request, but morally . . .'

The smile returned to Odal's face. 'You wish to monitor my thoughts. To record them and see how I perform during the duel. Interesting. Very interesting . . .'

The man at the door rose and said, 'If you have no desire for refreshments, gentlemen . . .'

Odal turned to him. 'Thank you for your attention.'

Their eyes met for an instant. The man gave a barely perceptible shake of his head, then left.

Odal returned his attention to Leoh. 'I'm sorry, Professor, but I can't allow you to monitor my thoughts during the duel.'

'But . . .'

'I regret having to refuse you. But, as you yourself pointed out, there is no legal requirement for such a course of action. I must refuse. I hope you understand.'

Leoh rose slowly from the couch. 'No, I do not understand. You sit here and discuss legal points when we both know full well that you're planning to murder Massan tomorrow.' His voice burning with anger, Leoh went on,

'You've turned my invention into a murder weapon. But you've turned me into an enemy. I'll find out how you're doing it, and I won't rest until you and your kind are put away where you belong ... on a planet for the criminally insane!'

Hector reached for the door and opened it. He and Leoh went out, leaving Odal alone in the room. In a few minutes, the dark-suited man returned.

'I have just spoken with the Leader on the tri-di and obtained permission to make a slight adjustment in our plans.'

'An adjustment, Minister Kor?'

'After your duel tomorrow, your next opponent will be Dr Leoh,' said Kor. 'He is the next man to die.'

*

The mists swirled deep and impenetrable around Fernd Massan. He stared blindly through the useless view plate in his helmet, then reached up slowly and carefully placed the infrared detector before his eyes.

I never realized a hallucination could seem so real, Massan thought.

Since the challenge by Odal, the actual world had seemed quite unreal. For a week, he had gone through the motions of life, but felt as though he were standing aside, a spectator mind watching its own body from a distance. The gathering of his friends and associates last night, the night before the duel – that silent, funereal group of people – it had all seemed completely unreal to him.

But now, in this manufactured dream, he seemed vibrantly alive. Every sensation was solid, stimulating. He could feel his pulse throbbing through him. Somewhere out in those mists, he knew, was Odal. And the thought of coming to grips with the assassin filled him with a strange satisfaction.

Massan had spent many years serving his government on the rich but inhospitable high-gravity planets of the Acquataine Cluster. This was the environment he had chosen:

49

crushing gravity; killing pressures; atmosphere of ammonia and hydrogen, laced with free radicals of sulphur and other valuable but deadly chemicals; oceans of liquid methane and ammonia; 'solid ground' consisting of quickly crumbling, eroding ice; howling, superpowerful winds that could pick up a mountain of ice and hurl it halfway around the planet; darkness; danger; death.

He was encased in a one-man protective outfit that was half armored suit, half vehicle. An internal liquid suspension system kept him tolerably comfortable at four times normal gravity, but still the suit was cumbersome, and a man could move only very slowly in it, even with the aid of servomotors.

The weapon he had chosen was simplicity itself: a hand-held capsule of oxygen. But in a hydrogen/ammonia atmosphere, oxygen could be a deadly explosive. Massan carried several of these 'bombs' hooked to his suit. So did Odal. *But the trick,* Massan thought to himself, *is to throw them accurately under these conditions; the proper range, the proper trajectory. Not an easy thing to learn, without years of experience.*

The terms of the duel were simple: Massan and Odal were situated on a rough-topped iceberg that was being swirled along one of the methane/ammonia ocean's vicious currents. The ice was rapidly crumbling. The duel was to end when the iceberg was completely broken up.

Massan edged along the ragged terrain. His suit's grippers and rollers automatically adjusted to the roughness of the topography. He concentrated his attention on the infrared detector that hung before his view plate.

A chunk of ice the size of a man's head sailed through the murky atmosphere in the steep glide peculiar to heavy gravity and banged into the shoulder of Massan's suit. The force was enough to rock him slightly off balance before the servos readjusted. Massan withdrew his arm from the sleeve and felt inside the shoulder seam. Dented, but not penetrated. A leak would have been disastrous, fatal. Then he remembered:

Of course, I cannot be killed except by the direct action of my antagonist. That is one of the rules of the game.

Still, he carefully fingered the shoulder seam to make certain it was not leaking. The dueling machine and its rules seemed so very remote and unsubstantial, compared to this freezing, howling inferno.

He diligently set about combing the iceberg, determined to find Odal and kill him before their floating island disintegrated. He thoroughly explored every projection, every crevice, every slope, working his way slowly from one end of the berg toward the other. Back and forth, cross and recross, with the infrared sensors scanning 360 degrees around him.

It was time-consuming. Even with the suit's servomotors and propulsion units, motion across the ice, against the buffeting wind, was a cumbersome business. But Massan continued to work his way across the iceberg, fighting down a gnawing, growing fear that Odal was not there at all.

And then he caught just the barest flicker of a shadow on his detector. Something, or someone, had darted behind a jutting rise of ice, off by the edge of the berg.

Slowly and carefully, Massan made his way across to the base of the rise. He picked one of the oxygen bombs from his belt and held it in his right-hand claw. Edging around the base of the ice cliff, he stood on a narrow ledge between the cliff and the churning sea. He saw no one. He extended the detector's range to maximum and worked the scanners up the sheer face of the cliff toward the top.

There he was! The shadowy outline of a man etched itself on his detector screen. And at the same time, Massan heard a muffled roar, then a rumbling, crashing noise, growing quickly louder and more menacing. He looked down the face of the ice cliff and saw a small avalanche of ice tumbling, sliding, growling toward him. *That devil set off a bomb at the top of the cliff!*

Massan tried to back out of the way, but it was too late.

The first chunk of ice bounced harmlessly off his helmet, but the others knocked him off balance so repeatedly that the servos had no chance to recover. He staggered blindly for a few moments, as more and more ice cascaded down on him, and then toppled off the ledge into the boiling sea.

Relax! he ordered himself. *Do not panic! The suit will float you. The servos will keep you right side up. You cannot be killed accidentally; Odal must perform the* coup de grâce *himself.*

There were emergency rockets on the back of the suit. If he could orient himself properly, a touch of the control stud on his belt would set them off and he would be boosted back onto the iceberg. He turned slightly inside the suit and tried to judge the iceberg's distance through the infrared detector. It was difficult, since the suit was bobbing madly in the churning currents.

Finally he decided to fire the rockets and make final adjustments of distance and landing site while he was in the air.

But he could not move his hand.

He tried, but his entire right arm was locked fast. He could not budge it a millimeter. And the same for the left. Something, or someone, was clamping his arms tight. He could not even pull them out of their sleeves.

Massan thrashed about, trying to shake off whatever it was. No use.

Then his detector screen was slowly lifted from the view plate. He felt something vibrating on his helmet. The oxygen tubes! They were being disconnected.

He screamed and tried to fight free. No use. With a hiss, the oxygen tubes pulled free of helmet. Massan could feel the blood pounding through his veins as he fought desperately to free himself.

Now he was being pushed down into the sea. He screamed again and tried to wrench his body away. The frothing sea filled his view plate. He was under. He was being held under.

And now . . . now the view plate itself was being loosened.

No! Don't! The scalding cold methane/ammonia sea seeped through the opening view plate.

'It's only a dream!' Massan shouted to himself. 'Only a dream! A dream! A . . .'

*

Dr Leoh stared at the dinner table without really seeing it. Coming to the restaurant had been Hector's idea. Three hours earlier Massan had been removed from the dueling machine – dead.

Leoh sat stolidly, hands in lap, his mind racing in many different directions at once. Hector was off at the phone, getting the lastest information from the meditechs. Odal had expressed his regrets perfunctorily, and then left for the Kerak embassy, under a heavy escort of his own plain-clothes guards. The government of the Acquataine Cluster was quite literally falling apart, with no man willing to assume the responsibility of leadership . . . and thereby expose himself. One hour after the duel, Kanus' troops had landed on all the major planets of Szarno; the annexation was complete.

And what have I done since I arrived here? Leoh demanded of himself. *Nothing. Absolutely nothing. I have sat back like a doddering old professor and played academic games with the machine, while younger, more vigorous, men have USED the machine to suit their own purposes.*

Used the machine. There was a fragment of an idea there. Something nebulous that must be approached carefully or it will fade away. Used the machine . . . used it . . . Leoh toyed with the phrase for a few moments, then gave it up with a sigh of resignation. *Lord, I'm too tired even to think.*

He focused his attention on his surroundings and scanned the busy dining room. It was a beautiful place, really, decorated with crystal and genuine woods and fabric draperies. Not a synthetic in sight. The odors of delicious food, the hushed murmur of polite conversation. The waiters and cooks and bus boys were humans, not the autocookers and servers that most restaurants employed. Leoh suddenly felt touched at Hector's attempt to restore his spirits – and at a junior lieutenant's salary.

He saw the young Watchman approaching the table, coming back from the phone. Hector bumped two waiters and stumbled over a chair before reaching the relative safety of his own seat.

'What's the verdict?' Leoh asked.

Hector's lean face was bleak. 'They couldn't revive him. Cerebral hemorrhage, the meditechs said ... brought on by shock.'

'Shock?'

'That's what they said. Something must've, um, overloaded his nervous system ... I guess.'

Leoh shook his head. 'I just don't understand any of this. I might as well admit it. I'm no closer to an answer now than when I arrived here. Perhaps I should have retired years ago, before the dueling machine was invented.'

'No ...'

'I mean it,' said Leoh. 'This is the first real intellectual problem I've had to contend with in years. Tinkering with machinery, that's easy. You know what you want and all you need is to make the machinery perform properly. But this ... I'm afraid I'm too old to handle a puzzle like this.'

Hector scratched his nose thoughtfully. Then he answered, 'If you can't handle the problem, sir, then we're going to have a war on our hands in a matter of months ... or maybe just weeks. I mean, Kanus won't be satisfied with swallowing the Szarno group. The Acquataine Cluster is next ... and he'll have to fight to get it.'

'Then the Star Watch will step in,' Leoh said.

Hunching forward in his chair in eagerness to make his point, Hector said, 'But ... look, it'll take time to mobilize the Star Watch. Kanus can move a lot faster than we can. Sure, we could throw in a task force, I mean, a token group. Kerak's army will chew them up pretty quick, though I ...

I'm no politician, but I think what'll happen is ... well, Kerak will gobble up the Acquataine Cluster and wipe out a Star Watch force in the process. Then we'll end up with the Commonwealth at war with Kerak. And that'll be a big war, because Kanus'll have Acquatainia's, uh, resources to draw on.'

Leoh began to answer, then stopped. His eyes were fixed on the far entrance of the dining-room. Suddenly every murmur in the busy restaurant stopped dead. Waiters stood frozen between tables. Eating, drinking, conversation hung suspended.

Hector turned in his chair and saw at the far entrance the slim, stiff, blue-uniformed figure of Odal.

The moment of silence passed. Everyone turned to his own business and avoided looking at the Kerak major. Odal, with a faint smile on his thin face, made his way slowly to the table where Hector and Leoh were sitting.

They rose to greet him and exchanged perfunctory salutations. Odal pulled up a chair and sat with them, unasked.

'What do you want?' Leoh asked curtly.

Before Odal could reply, the waiter assigned to the table walked up, took a position where his back would be to the Kerak major, and asked firmly, 'Your dinner is ready, gentlemen. Shall I serve it now?'

'Yes,' Hector said before Leoh could speak. 'The major will be leaving shortly.'

Again the tight grin pulled across Odal's face. The waiter bowed and left.

'I've been thinking about our conversation of last night,' Odal said to Leoh.

'Yes?'

'You accused me of cheating in my duels.'

Leoh's eyebrows arched. 'I said someone was cheating ...'

'An accusation is an accusation.'

Leoh said nothing.

'Do you withdraw your words, or do you still accuse me

of deliberate murder? I'm willing to allow you to apologize and leave Acquatainia in peace.'

Hector cleared his throat noisily. 'This is no place for an argument ... besides, here comes our dinner.'

Odal ignored the Watchman, kept his ice-blue eyes fastened on Leoh. 'You heard me, Professor. Will you leave? Or do you ...'

Hector banged his fist on the table and jerked up out of his chair – just as the waiter arrived with a heavy tray of appetizers and soups. There was a loud crash. A tureen of soup, two bowls of salad, glasses, assorted rolls, cheese, and other delicacies cascaded over Odal.

The Kerak major leaped to his feet, swearing violently in his own language. The restaurant exploded with laughter.

Sputtering back into basic Terran, Odal shouted, 'You clumsy, stupid oaf! You maggot-brained misbegotten peasant-faced ...'

Hector calmly picked a salad leaf from the sleeve of his tunic, while Odal's voice choked with rage.

'I guess I am clumsy,' Hector said, grinning. 'As for being stupid, and the rest of it, I resent that. In fact, I'm highly insulted.'

A flash of recognition lighted Odal's eyes. 'I see. Of course. My quarrel is not with you. I apologize.' He turned back to Leoh, who was also standing now.

'Not good enough,' Hector said. 'I don't, uh, like the tone of your apology ... I mean ...'

Leoh raised a hand as if to warn Hector to be silent.

'I apologized,' Odal said, his face red with anger. 'That is enough.'

Hector took a step toward Odal. 'I guess I could call you names, or insult your glorious Leader, or something like that ... but this seems more direct.' He took the water pitcher from the table and carefully poured it over Odal's head.

The people in the restaurant roared. Odal went absolutely

white. 'You are determined to die.' He wiped the dripping water from his eyes. 'I'll meet you before the week is out. And you've saved no one.' He turned and stalked out.

Everyone else in the room stood up and applauded. Hector bobbed his head and grinned.

Aghast, Leoh asked 'Do you realize what you've done?'

'He was going to challenge you ...'

'He'll still challenge me, after you're dead.'

Shrugging, Hector said, 'Well, yes, maybe so. I guess you're right. But at least we've gained a little more time.'

'Four days.' Leoh shook his head. 'Four days to the end of this week. All right, come on, we have work to do.'

Hector was grinning broadly as they left the restaurant. He began to whistle.

'What are you so happy about?' Leoh grumbled.

'About you, sir. When we came in here, you were, well ... almost beaten. Now you're right back in the game again.'

Leoh stared at him. 'In your own odd way, my boy, you're quite something ... I think.'

*

Their ground car glided from the parking building to the restaurant's entrance ramp, at the radio call of the doorman. Within minutes, Hector and Leoh were cruising through the city in the deepening shadows of night.

'There's only one man,' Leoh mused, 'who's faced Odal and lived through it.'

'Dulaq,' Hector said. 'But ... he might as well be dead, for all the information anybody can get from him.'

'He's still completely withdrawn?'

Hector nodded. 'The medicos think that ... well, maybe with drugs and therapy and all that ... maybe in a few months or so they might be able to bring him back.'

'Not soon enough. We've only got four days.'

'I know.'

Leoh was silent for several minutes. Then, 'Who is Dulaq's closest living relative? Does he have a wife?'

'Umm, I think his wife's dead. Has a daughter, though. Pretty girl. I bumped into her in the hospital once or twice...'

Leoh smiled in the darkness. Hector's term, 'bumped into,' was probably completely literal.

'There might be a way to make Dulaq tell us what happened during his duel,' Leoh said. 'But it's a very dangerous way. Perhaps a fatal way.'

Hector didn't reply.

'Come on, my boy,' Leoh said. 'Let's find that daughter and talk to her.'

'Tonight?'

'Now.'

She certainly is a pretty girl, Leoh thought as he explained very carefully to Geri Dulaq what he proposed to do. She sat quietly and politely in the spacious living room of the Dulaq residence. The glittering chandelier cast touches of fire on her chestnut hair. Her slim body was slightly rigid with tension, her hands were clasped tightly in her lap. Her face, which looked as though it could be very expressive, was completely serious now.

'And that's the sum of it,' Leoh concluded. 'I believe that it will be possible to use the dueling machine itself to examine your father's thoughts and determine what took place during his duel against Major Odal. It might even help to break him out of his coma.'

She asked softly, 'But it might also be such a shock to him that he could die?'

Leoh nodded wordlessly.

'Then I'm very sorry, Professor, but I must say no.' Firmly.

'I understand your feelings,' Leoh replied, 'but I hope you realize that unless we can stop Odal immediately, we may very well be faced with war, and millions will die.'

She nodded. 'I know. But we're speaking of my father's

life. Kanus will have his war in any event, no matter what I do.'

'Perhaps,' Leoh admitted. 'Perhaps.'

Hector and Leoh drove back to the university campus and their quarters in the dueling machine building. Neither of them slept well that night.

The next morning, after an unenthusiastic breakfast, they found themselves in the antiseptic-white chamber, before the looming impersonal intricacy of the machine.

'Would you like to practice with it?' Leoh asked.

Hector shook his head gloomily. 'Maybe later.'

The phone chimed in Leoh's office. They both went in. Geri Dulaq's face took form on the view screen.

'I just heard the news,' she said a little breathlessly. 'I didn't know, last night, that Lieutenant Hector had challenged Odal.'

'He challenged Odal,' Leoh answered, 'to prevent the assassin from challenging me.'

'Oh.' Her face was a mixture of concern and reluctance. 'You're a brave man, Lieutenant.'

Hector's expression went through a dozen contortions, all of them speechless.

'Won't you reconsider your decision?' Leoh asked. 'Hector's life may depend on it.'

She closed her eyes briefly, then said, 'I can't. My father's life is my first responsibility. I'm sorry.' There was real torment in her voice.

They exchanged a few meaningless trivialities – with Hector still thoroughly tongue-tied – and ended the conversation on a polite but strained note.

Leoh rubbed his thumb across the phone switch for a moment, then turned to Hector. 'My boy, I think it would be a good idea for you to go straight to the hospital and check on Dulaq's condition.'

'But ... why ...'

59

'Don't argue, son. This could be vitally important. Check on Dulaq. In person, no phone calls.'

Hector shrugged and left the office. Leoh sat down at his desk and waited. There was nothing else he could do. After a while he got up and paced out to the big chamber, through the main doors, and out onto the campus. He walked past a dozen buildings, turned and strode as far as the decorative fence that marked the end of the main campus, ignoring students and faculty alike. He walked all around the campus, like a picket, trading nervous energy for time.

As he approached the dueling machine building again he spotted Hector walking dazedly toward him. For once, the Watchman was not whistling. Leoh cut across some lawn to get to him.

'Well?' he asked.

Hector shook his head, as if to clear away an inner fog. 'How did you know she'd be at the hospital?'

'The wisdom of age. What happened?'

'She kissed me. Right there in the hallway of the . . .'

'Spare me the geography,' Leoh cut in. 'What did she say?'

'I bumped into her in the hallway. We, uh, started talking . . . sort of. She seemed, well . . . worried about me. She got upset. Emotional. You know? I guess I looked pretty down . . . I mean, I'm not that brave . . . I'm scared and it must have shown.'

'You aroused her maternal instinct.'

'I . . . I don't think it was that . . . exactly. Well, anyway, she said that if I'm willing to risk my life to save yours, she couldn't protect her father any more. Said she was doing it out of selfishness, really, since he's her only living relative . . . I don't believe she meant it, but she said it anyway.'

They had reached the building by now. Leoh grabbed Hector's arm and steered him clear of a collision with the half-open door.

'She's agreed to let us put Dulaq in the dueling machine?'

'Sort of.'

'Eh?'

'The medical staff doesn't want him moved ... especially not back here. She agrees with them.'

Leoh snorted. 'All right. In fact, so much the better. I'd rather not have the Kerak people see us bring Dulaq to the dueling machine. Instead, we'll smuggle the dueling machine into the hospital!'

*

They plunged to work immediately. Leoh preferred not to inform the regular staff of the dueling machine about their plan, so he and Hector had to work through the night and most of the next morning. Hector barely understood what he was doing, but with Leoh's supervision he managed to dismantle part of the machine's central network, insert a few additional black electronics boxes that the Professor had conjured up from the spare-parts bins in the basement, and then reconstruct the machine so that it looked exactly the same as before they had started.

In between his frequent trips to oversee Hector's work, Leoh had jury-rigged a rather bulky headset and a hand-sized override control circuit. The late morning sun was streaming through the hall when Leoh finally explained it all to Hector.

'A simple matter of technological improvisation,' he told the puzzled Watchman. 'You've installed a short-range transceiver into the machine, and this headset is a portable transceiver for Dulaq. Now he can sit in his hospital bed and still be "in" the dueling machine.'

Only the three most trusted members of the hospital staff were taken into Leoh's confidence, and they were hardly enthusiastic about the plan.

'It is a waste of time,' said the chief psychotechnician, shaking his white-maned head vigorously. 'You cannot expect a patient who has shown no positive response to drugs and therapy to respond to your machine.'

Leoh argued, and Geri Dulaq firmly insisted that they go

through with it. Finally the doctors agreed. With only two days remaining before Hector's duel with Odal, they began to probe Dulaq's mind. Geri remained by her father's bedside while the three doctors fitted the cumbersome transceiver to his head and attached the electrodes for the hospital equipment that monitored his physical condition. Hector and Leoh remained at the dueling machine, communicating with the hospital by phone.

Leoh made a final check of the controls and circuitry, then put in the last call to the tense little group in Dulaq's room. All was ready.

He walked out to the machine with Hector beside him. Their footsteps echoed hollowly in the sepulchral chamber. Leoh stopped at the nearer booth.

'Now remember,' he said carefully, 'I'll be holding the emergency control unit in my hand. It will stop the duel the instant I set it off. However, if something goes wrong, you must be prepared to act quickly. Keep a close watch on my physical condition; I've shown you which instruments to check on the control board.'

'Yes, sir.'

Leoh nodded and took a deep breath. 'Very well, then.'

He stepped into the booth and sat down. Hector helped to attach the neurocontacts, and then left him alone. Leoh leaned back and waited for the semihypnotic effect to take hold. Dulaq's choice of the city and the stat-wand were known. But beyond that, everything was sealed in his uncommunicating mind. Could the machine reach past that seal?

Slowly, lullingly, the dueling machine's imaginary yet very real mists enveloped Leoh. When they cleared, he was standing on the upper pedestrian level of the main commercial street of the city. For a long moment, everything was still.

Have I made contact? Whose eyes am I seeing with, my own or Dulaq's?

And then he sensed it – an amused, somewhat astonished marveling at the reality of the illusion. Dulaq's thoughts!

Make your mind a blank, Leoh told himself. *Watch. Listen. Be passive.*

He became a spectator, seeing and hearing the world through Dulaq's eyes and ears as the Acquatainian Prime Minister advanced through his nightmarish ordeal. He felt the confusion, frustration, apprehension, and growing terror as, time and again, Odal appeared in the crowd – only to melt into someone else and escape.

The first part of the duel ended, and Leoh was suddenly buffeted by a jumble of thoughts and impressions. Then the thoughts slowly cleared and steadied.

Leoh saw an immense and totally barren plain. Not a tree, not a blade of grass, nothing but bare, rocky ground stretching in all directions to the horizon and a disturbingly harsh yellow sky. At his feet was the weapon Odal had chosen. A primitive club.

He shared Dulaq's sense of dread as he picked up the club and hefted it. Off on the horizon he could see the tall lithe figure holding a similar club and walking toward him.

Despite himself, Leoh could feel his own excitement. He had broken through the shock-created armor that Dulaq's mind had erected! Dulaq was reliving the part of the duel that had caused the shock.

Reluctantly, he advanced to meet Odal. But as they drew closer together, the one figure of his opponent seemed to split apart. Now there were two, four, six of them. Six Odals, six mirror images, all armed with massive, evil clubs, advancing steadily on him. Six tall, lean, blond assassins with six cold smiles on their intent faces.

Horrified, completely panicked, he scrambled away trying to evade the six opponents with the half-dozen clubs raised and poised to strike.

Their young legs easily outdistanced him. A smash on his back sent him sprawling. One of them kicked his weapon away.

They stood over him for a malevolent, gloating second.

Then six strong arms flashed down, again and again, mercilessly. Pain and blood, screaming agony, punctuated by the awful thudding of solid clubs hitting fragile flesh and bone, over and over again, endlessly, endlessly . . .

Everything went blank.

Leoh opened his eyes and saw Hector bending over him.

'Are you all right, sir?'

'I . . . I think so.'

'The controls hit the danger mark all at once. You were . . . well, you were screaming.'

'I don't doubt it,' Leoh said.

They walked, with Leoh leaning on Hector's arm, from the dueling machine to the office.

'That was . . . an experience,' Leoh said, easing himself onto the couch.

'What happened? What did Odal do? What made Dulaq go into shock? How does . . .'

The old man silenced Hector with a wave of his hand. 'One question at a time, please.'

Leoh leaned back on the deep couch and told Hector every detail of both parts of the duel.

'Six Odals,' Hector muttered soberly, leaning against the doorframe. 'Six against one.'

'That's what he did. It's easy to see how a man expecting a polite, formal duel can be completely shattered by the viciousness of such an attack. And the machine amplifies every impulse, every sensation.' Leoh shuddered.

'But how does he do it?' Hector's voice was suddenly demanding.

'I've been asking myself the same question. We've checked the dueling machine time and again. There's no possible way for Odal to plug in five helpers . . . unless . . .'

'Unless?'

Leoh hesitated, seemingly debating with himself. Finally he nodded sharply and answered, 'Unless Odal is a telepath.'

'Telepath? But . . .'

64

'I know it sounds farfetched, but there have been well-documented cases of telepathy.'

Frowning, Hector said, 'Sure, everybody's heard about it ... natural telepaths, I mean ... but they're so unpredictable ... I mean, how can ...'

Leoh leaned forward on the couch and clasped his hands in front of his chin. 'The Terran races have never developed telepathy, or any extrasensory talents, beyond the occasional wild talent. They never had to, not with tri-di communications and star ships. But perhaps the Kerak people are different ...'

'They're human, just like we are,' Hector said. 'Besides, if they had, uh, telepathic abilities ... well, wouldn't they use them all the time? Why just in the dueling machine?'

'Of course!' Leoh exclaimed. 'Odal's shown telepathic ability only in the dueling machine!'

Hector blinked.

Excitedly, Leoh explained, 'Suppose Odal's a natural telepath ... the same as dozens of Terrans have been proven to be. He has an erratic, difficult-to-control talent. A talent that doesn't really amount to much. Then he gets into the dueling machine. The machine amplifies his thoughts. It also amplifies his talents!'

'Ohhh.'

'You see? Outside the machine, he's no better than any wandering fortuneteller. But the dueling machine gives his natural abilities the amplification and reproducibility that they could never attain unaided.'

'I get it.'

'So it's a fairly straightforward matter for him to have five associates in the Kerak embassy sit in on the duel, so to speak. Possibly they're natural telepaths, too, but they needn't be.'

'They just, uh, pool their minds with his? Six men show up in the duel ... pretty nasty.' Hector dropped into the desk chair. 'So what do we do now?'

'Now?' Leoh blinked at the Watchman. 'Why ... I

suppose the first thing we do is call the hospital and see how Dulaq came through.'

'Oh, yes ... I forgot about her ... I mean, him.'

Leoh put the call through. Geri Dulaq's face appeared on the screen, impassive.

'How is he?' Hector blurted.

'It was too much for him,' she said bleakly. 'He is dead. The doctors have tried to revive him, but ...'

'No.' Leoh groaned.

'I'm ... sorry,' Hector said. 'I'll be right down there. Stay where you are.'

The Star Watchman dashed out of the office as Geri broke the phone connection. Leoh stared at the blank screen for a few minutes, then leaned far back in the couch and closed his eyes. He was suddenly exhausted, physically and emotionally. He fell asleep, and dreamed of men dead and dying. Sometimes it was Odal killing them, and sometimes it was Leoh himself.

Hector's nerve-shattering whistling woke him up. It was deep night outside.

'What are you so happy about?' Leoh groused as Hector popped in to the office.

'Happy? Me?'

'You were whistling.'

Hector shrugged. 'I always whistle, sir. Doesn't mean I'm happy.'

'All right.' Leoh rubbed his eyes. 'How did the girl take her father's death?'

'Pretty hard. She cried a lot. It ... well, it shook us both up.'

Leoh looked at the younger man. 'Does she blame ... me?'

'You? Why, no, sir. Why should she? Odal, Kanus ... the Kerak Worlds. But not you.'

The Professor sighed, relieved. 'Very well. Now then, we have much work to do, and little time to do it in.'

'What do you want me to do?' Hector asked.

'Phone the Star Watch Commander . . .'

'My Commanding officer, all the way back at Perseus Alpha VI? That's a hundred light-years from here.'

'No, no, no,' Leoh shook his head. 'The Commander-in-Chief, Sir Harold Spencer. At Star Watch Central Headquarters, or wherever he may be, no matter how far. Get through to him as quickly as possible. And reverse the charges.'

With a low whistle of astonishment, Hector began punching buttons on the phone.

*

The morning of the duel arrived, and precisely at the specified hour, Odal and a small retinue of Kerak seconds stepped through the double doors of the dueling machine chamber.

Hector and Leoh were already there, waiting. With them stood another man, dressed in the black-and-silver of the Star Watch. He was a blocky, broad-faced veteran with iron-gray hair and hard, unsmiling eyes.

The two little groups of men knotted together in the center of the room, before the machine's main control board. The white-uniformed staff meditechs emerged from a far doorway and stood off to one side.

Odal went through the formality of shaking hands with Hector. The Kerak major nodded toward the older Watchman. 'Your replacement?' he asked mischievously.

The chief meditech stepped between them. 'Since you are the challenged party, Major Odal, you have the first choice of weapon and environment. Are there any instructions or comments necessary before the duel begins?'

'I think not,' Odal replied. 'The situation will be self-explanatory. I assume, of course, that Star Watchmen are trained to be warriors and not merely technicians. The situation I have chosen is one in which many warriors have won glory.'

Hector said nothing.

'I intend,' Leoh said firmly, 'to assist the staff in monitoring this duel. Your aides may, of course, sit at the control board with me.'

Odal nodded.

'If you are ready to begin, gentlemen,' the chief meditech said.

Hector and Odal went to their booths. Leoh sat at the control console, and one of the Kerak men sat down next to him. The others found places on the long curving bench that faced the machine.

Hector felt every nerve and muscle tensed as he sat in the booth, despite his efforts to relax. Slowly the tension eased and he began to feel slightly drowsy. The booth seemed to be melting away ...

Hector heard a snuffling noise behind him and wheeled around. He blinked, then stared.

It had four legs, and was evidently a beast of burden. At least, it carried a saddle on its back. Piled atop the saddle was a conglomeration of what looked to Hector – at first glance – like a pile of junk. He went over to the animal and examined it carefully. The 'junk' turned out to be a long spear, various pieces of armor, a helmet, sword, shield, battle-ax and dagger.

The situation I have chosen is one in which many warriors have won glory.

Hector puzzled over the assortment of weapons. They came straight out of Kerak's Dark Age. Probably Odal had been practicing with them for months, even years. *He may not need five helpers*, Hector thought.

Warily, he put on the armor. The breastplate seemed too big, and he was somehow unable to tighten the greaves on his shins properly. The helmet fit over his head like an ancient oil can, flattening his ears and nose and forcing him to squint to see through the narrow eye slit. Finally he buckled on the sword and found attachments on the saddle for the other weapons. The shield was almost too heavy to lift, and he barely struggled into the saddle with all the weight he was carrying.

And then he just sat. He began to feel a little ridiculous. *Suppose it rains?* But of course it wouldn't.

After an interminable wait, Odal appeared on a powerful trotting charger. His armor was black as space, and so was his mount. *Naturally,* thought Hector.

Odal saluted gravely with his great spear from across the meadow. Hector returned the salute, nearly dropping his spear in the process.

Then Odal lowered his spear and aimed it – so it seemed to Hector – directly at the Watchman's ribs. He pricked his mount into a canter. Hector did the same, and his steed jogged into a bumping, jolting gallop. The two warriors hurtled toward each other from opposite ends of the meadow, with Hector barely hanging on to his mount.

And suddenly there were six black figures roaring down on Hector!

The Watchman's stomach wrenched within him. Automatically he tried to turn his mount aside. But the beast had no intention of going anywhere except straight ahead. The Kerak warriors bore in, six abreast, with six spears aimed menacingly.

Abruptly, Hector heard the pounding of other hoof-beats right beside him. Through a corner of his helmet slit he glimpsed at least two other warriors charging with him into Odal's crew.

Leoh's gamble had worked. The transceiver that had allowed Dulaq to make contact with the dueling machine from his hospital bed was now allowing five Star Watch officers to join Hector, even though they were physically sitting in a star ship orbiting high above the planet.

The odds were even now. The five additional Watchmen were the roughest, hardiest, most aggressive man-to-man fighters that the Star Watch could provide on one-day's notice.

Twelve powerful chargers met head-on, and twelve strong men smashed together with an ear-splitting CLANG! Shattered spears showered splinters everywhere. Men and animals went down.

Hector was rocked back in his saddle, but somehow managed to avoid falling off. On the other hand, he couldn't really regain his balance, either. Dust and weapons filled the air. A sword hissed near his head and rattled off his shield.

With a supreme effort, Hector pulled out his own sword and thrashed at the nearest rider. It turned out to be a fellow Watchman, but the stroke bounced harmlessly off his helmet.

It was so confusing. The wheeling, snorting animals. Clouds of dust. Screaming, raging men. A black-armored rider charged into Hector, waving a battle-ax over his head. He chopped savagely, and the Watchman's shield split apart. Another frightening swing – Hector tried to duck and slid completely out of the saddle, thumping painfully on the ground, while the ax cleaved the air where his head had been a split second earlier.

Somehow his helmet was turned around. Hector tried to decide whether to grope around blindly or lay down his sword and straighten out the helmet. The problem was solved for him by the *crang*! of a sword against the back of his head. The blow flipped him into a somersault, and knocked the helmet off completely.

Hector climbed painfully to his feet, his head spinning. It took him several moments to realize that the battle had stopped.

The dust drifted away, and he saw that all the Kerak fighters were down – except one. The black-armored warrior took off his helmet and tossed it aside. It was Odal. Or was it? They all looked alike. *What difference does it make?* Hector wondered. *Odal's mind is the dominant one.*

Odal stood, legs braced apart, sword in hand, and looked uncertainly at the other Star Watchmen. Three of them were afoot and two still mounted. The Kerak major seemed as confused as Hector felt. The shock of facing equal numbers had sapped much of his confidence.

Cautiously he advanced toward Hector, holding his sword out before him. The other Watchmen stood aside while Hector slowly backpedaled, stumbling slightly on the uneven ground.

Odal feinted and cut at Hector's arm. The Watchman barely parried in time. Another feint, at the head, and a slash to the chest; Hector missed the parry but his armor saved him. Odal kept advancing. Feint, feint, crack! Hector's sword went flying from his hand.

For the barest instant everyone froze. Then Hector leaped desperately straight at Odal, caught him completely by surprise, and wrestled him to the ground. The Watchman pulled the sword from Odal's hand and tossed it away. But with his free hand Odal clouted Hector on the side of the head and knocked him on his back. Both men scrambled up and ran for the nearest weapons.

Odal picked up a wicked-looking double-bladed ax. One of the mounted Star Watchmen handed Hector a huge broadsword. He gripped it with both hands, but still staggered off balance as he swung it up over his shoulder.

Holding the broadsword aloft, Hector charged toward Odal, who stood dogged, short-breathed, sweat-streaked, waiting for him. The broadsword was quite heavy, even for a two-handed grip. And Hector never noticed his own battered helmet lying on the ground between them.

Odal, for his part, had Hector's charge and swing timed perfectly in his own mind. He would duck under the swing and bury his ax in the Watchman's chest. Then he would face the others. Probably, with their leader gone, the duel would automatically end. But, of course, Hector would not really be dead; the best Odal could hope for now was to win the duel.

Hector charged directly into Odal's plan, but the Watchman's timing was much poorer than anticipated. Just as he began the downswing of a mighty broadsword stroke, he stumbled on the helmet. Odal started to duck, then saw the Watchman was diving face-first into the ground, legs flailing, and that heavy broadsword was cleaving through the air with a will of its own.

Odal pulled back in confusion, only to have the wild-swinging broadsword strike him just above the wrist with bone-shattering impact. The ax dropped out of his hand and Odal involuntarily grasped the wounded forearm with his left hand. Blood seeped through his fingers.

Shaking his head in bitter resignation, Odal turned his back on the prostrate Hector and began walking away.

Slowly the scene faded, and Hector found himself sitting in the booth of the dueling machine.

*

The door opened and Leoh squeezed into the booth.

'You're all right?'

Hector blinked and refocused his eyes on reality. 'I think so . . .'

'Everything went well? The Watchmen got through to you?'

'Good thing they did. I was nearly killed anyway.'

'But you survived.'

'So far.'

Across the room, Odal stood massaging his forearm while Kor demanded, 'How could they possibly have discovered the secret? Where was the leak? Who spoke to them?'

'That's not important now,' Odal said quietly. 'The primary fact is that they've not only discovered our trick, but they've found a way to duplicate it.'

The glistening dome of Kor's bullet-shaped head – which barely rose to the level of Odal's chin – was glowing with rage.

'The sanctimonious hypocrites,' Kor snarled, 'accusing us of cheating, and then they do the very same thing.'

'Regardless of the moral values of our mutual behavior,' Odal said dryly, 'it's evident that there's no longer any use in calling on telepathically guided assistants. I'll face the Watchman alone during the second half of the duel.'

'Can you trust them to do the same?'

'Yes. They easily defeated my aides, then stood aside and allowed the two of us to fight by ourselves.'

'And you failed to defeat him?'

Odal frowned. 'I was wounded by a fluke. He's a very ... unusual opponent. I can't decide whether he's actually as clumsy as he appears, or whether he's shamming and trying to confuse me. Either way, it's impossible to predict what he's going to do.' To himself he added, *Could he be telepathic, also?*

Kor's gray eyes became flat and emotionless. 'You know, of course, how the Leader will react if you fail to kill this Watchman. Not merely defeat him. He must be killed. The aura of invincibility must be maintained.'

'I'll do my best,' Odal said.

'He must be killed.'

The chime that marked the end of the rest period sounded. Odal and Hector returned to their booths. Now it was Hector's choice of environment and weapons.

Odal found himself enveloped in darkness. Only gradually did his eyes adjust. He was in a spacesuit. For several minutes he stood motionless, peering into the darkness, every sense alert, every muscle coiled for instant action. Dimly he could see the outlines of jagged rock against a background of innumerable stars. Experimentally, he lifted one foot. It stuck, tacky, to the surface. *Magnetized boots. This must be a planetoid.*

As his eyes grew accustomed to the dimness he saw that he was right. It was a small planetoid, perhaps a mile or so in diameter, he judged. Almost zero gravity. Airless.

Odal swiveled his head inside the fish-bowl helmet of his suit and saw, over his right shoulder, the figure of Hector –

lank and ungainly even with the bulky suit. For a moment, Odal puzzled over the weapon to be used. Then Hector bent down, picked up a loose stone, straightened, and tossed it softly past Odal's head. He watched it sail by and off into the darkness of space, never to return. A warning shot.

Pebbles? Odal thought to himself. *Pebbles for a weapon? He must be insane.* Then he remembered that inertial mass was unaffected by gravity, or the lack of it. On this planetoid a fifty-kilogram rock might be easier to carry, but it would be just as hard to throw – and it would do just as much damage when it hit, regardless of its gravitational 'weight'.

Odal crouched down and selected a stone the size of his fist. He rose carefully, sighted Hector standing a hundred meters or so away, and threw as hard as he could.

The effort of his throw sent him tumbling off balance and the stone was far off target. He fell to his hands and knees, bounced lightly, and skipped to a stop. Immediately he drew his feet up under his body and planted the magnetized shoes of his boots firmly on the iron-rich surface.

But before he could stand again, a small stone *pinged* lightly off his oxygen tank. The Star Watchman had his range already! Probably he had spent some time on planetoids. Odal scrambled to the nearest upjutting rocks and crouched behind them. *Lucky I didn't rip open the suit,* he told himself. Three stones, evidently hurled in salvo, ticked off the top of the rock he was hunched behind. One of the stones bounced off his fish-bowl helmet.

Odal scooped up a handful of pebbles and tossed them in Hector's general direction. *That should make him duck. Perhaps he'll stumble and crack his helmet open.*

He grinned at that. *That's it. Kor wants him dead, and that's the way to do it. Pin him under a big rock, then bury him alive under more rocks. A few at a time, stretched out nicely. Break some of his bones in the process, and let him sweat while his oxygen supply runs out. That should put enough strain on his nervous system to hospitalize him, at* least. Then he can be assassinated by more conventional means. Perhaps he'll even be as obliging as Massan, and have a fatal stroke.

A large rock. One that's light enough to lift and throw, yet also big enough to pin him for a few moments. Once he's down, it will be easy enough to bury him under more rocks.

Odal spotted a boulder of the proper size, a few meters away. He backed toward it throwing small stones in Hector's direction to keep the Watchman busy. In return, a barrage of stones began striking all around him. Several hit him, one hard enough to knock him slightly off balance.

Slowly, patiently Odal reached his chosen weapon: an oblong boulder, about the size of a small chair. He crouched behind it and tugged at it experimentally. It moved slightly. Another stone zinged off his arm, hard enough to hurt. Odal could see Hector clearly now, standing atop a small rise, calmly firing stones at him. He smiled as he coiled cat-like, and tensed himself. He gripped the boulder with his outstretched arms and hands.

Then in one vicious uncoiling motion he snatched it up, whirled around, and hurled it at Hector. The violence of the action sent him tottering awkwardly as he released the boulder. He fell to the ground, but kept his eyes fixed on the boulder as it tumbled end over end, directly at the Watchman.

For an eternally long instant Hector stood motionless, seemingly entranced. Then he leaped sideways, floating dream-like in the low gravity as the stone bore inexorably past him.

Odal pounded his fist on the ground in fury. He started up, only to have a good-sized stone slam against his shoulder and knock him flat again. He looked up in time to see Hector fire again. A stone puffed into the ground inches from Odal's helmet. The Kerak major flattened himself. Several more stones clattered on his helmet and oxygen tank. Then nothing.

Odal looked up and saw Hector squatting, reaching for more ammunition. The Kerak warrior stood up quickly, his own fists filled with stones. He cocked his arm to throw ...

Something made him turn around and look behind him. The boulder loomed before his eyes, still tumbling slowly as it had when he'd thrown it. It was too big and too close to avoid. It smashed into Odal, picked him off his feet, and slammed him against the upjutting rocks a few meters away.

Even before he began to feel the pain inside him, Odal began trying to push the boulder off. But he couldn't get enough leverage. Then he saw the Star Watchman's form standing over him.

'I didn't really think you'd fall for it,' Hector's voice said in his earphones. 'I mean ... didn't you realize that the boulder was too massive to escape completely after it missed me? You just threw it into orbit ... uh, a two-minute orbit, roughly. It *had* to come back ... all I had to do was keep you in the same spot for a few minutes.'

Odal said nothing, but strained every cell in his pain-racked body to get the boulder off him. Hector reached over his shoulder and began fumbling with the valves that were pressed against the rocks.

'Sorry to do this ... but I'm not killing you ... just defeating you. Let's see, one of these is the oxygen valve and the other, I think, is the emergency rocket pack. Now which is which?'

Hector's hand tightened on a valve and turned it sharply. A rocket roared to life and Odal was hurtled free of the boulder, shot completely off the planetoid. Hector was bowled over by the blast and rolled halfway around the tiny chunk of rock and metal.

Odal tried to reach the rocket throttle, but the pain was too great. He was slipping into unconsciousness. He fought against it. He knew he must return to the planetoid and somehow kill his opponent. But gradually the pain overpowered him. His eyes were closing, closing ...

And quite abruptly he found himself sitting in the booth

of the dueling machine. It took a moment for him to realize that he was back in the real world. Then his thoughts cleared. He had failed to kill Hector. He hadn't even defeated him.

And at the door of the booth stood Kor, his face a grim mask of anger.

*

For the moment, Leoh's office behind the dueling machine looked like a great double room. One wall had been replaced by a full-sized view screen, which now seemed to be dissolved, so that he was looking directly into the austere metallic utility of a star-ship compartment.

Spencer was saying, 'So this hired assassin, after killing four men and nearly wrecking a government, has returned to his native worlds.'

Leoh nodded. 'He returned under guard. I suppose he's in disgrace, or perhaps even under arrest.'

'Servants of a dictator never know when they'll be the ones who are served – on a platter.' Spencer chuckled. 'And the Watchman who assisted you, this Junior Lieutenant Hector, where is he?'

'The Dulaq girl has him in tow, somewhere. Evidently it's the first time he's been a hero.'

Spencer shifted his weight in his chair. 'I've long prided myself on the conviction that any Star Watch officer can handle almost any kind of emergency. From your description of the past few weeks' happenings, I was beginning to have my doubts. However, Junior Lieutenant Hector seems to have scraped through.'

'He turned out to be an extremely valuable man,' Leoh said, smiling. 'I think he'll make a fine officer.'

Spencer grunted an affirmative.'

'Well,' Leoh said, 'that's the story, to date. I believe that Odal is finished. But the Kerak Worlds have annexed the Szarno Confederacy and are rearming in earnest now. And the Acquatainian government is still very wobbly. There will be elections for a new Prime Minister in a few days, with half a dozen men running and no one in a clear majority. We haven't heard the last of Kanus, either, not by a long shot.'

Spencer lifted a shaggy eyebrow. 'Neither,' he rumbled, 'has *he* heard the last from *us*.'

The Force of Pride

Odal sat alone in the waiting room. It was a bare cubicle, with rough stone walls and a single slit window set high above the floor, close to the ceiling. For furniture, there was only one wooden bench and a view screen set into the wall opposite it. The room was quiet as death.

The Kerak major sat stiff-backed and unmoving. But his mind was racing.

Kor uses this type of room to awe his visitors. He knows how much like an ancient dungeon this room looks. He likes to terrify people.

Odal also knew that the interrogation rooms, deep in the sub-basements, were also built like this. Except that they had no windows, and the walls were often blood-spattered.

'The Minister will see you now,' said a feminine voice from the view screen. But the screen remained blank. Odal realized that he had probably been under observation every minute since he had entered Kor's headquarters.

He stood up as the room's only door opened automatically. With a measured military briskness, Odal strode down the hallway toward the other door at its end, his boots clicking on the stone flooring. He knocked once at the heavy wooden door. No answer. He knocked again, and the door opened by itself.

Kor was sitting at the far end of the office, behind a mammoth desk. The room was dimly lit, except for a single lamp over the desk that made the Intelligence Minister's bald head glisten. Odal carefully shut the door, took a few steps into the carpeted room, and waited for Kor to look up. The Intelligence chief was busily signing papers, ignoring his visitor.

Finally Kor glanced up. 'Sit,' he commanded.

Odal walked to the desk and sat at the single straight-backed chair before it. Kor signed a few more documents, then pushed the stack of papers off to the side of his desk.

'I spent the morning with the Leader,' he said in his irritatingly shrill voice. 'Needless to say, he was unhappy about your duel with the Watchman.'

Odal could picture Kanus' angry tirade. 'My only desire is to meet the Watchman again and rectify that error.'

Kor's emotionless eyes fixed on Odal's. 'Personal motives are of no interest. The Watchman is only a bumbling fool, but he has succeeded in destroying our primary plan for the defeat of Acquatainia. He succeeded because of this meddler, Leoh. *He* is our target. He is the one who must be put out of the way.'

'I see . . .'

'No, you do not see,' Kor snapped. 'You have no concept of the plan I have in mind, because I have told it to no one except the Leader himself. And I will tell it to no one, until it is necessary.'

Odal didn't move a muscle. He refused to show any emotion, any fear, any weakness to his superior.

'For the time being you are assigned to my personal staff. You will remain at this headquarters building at all times. Your duties will be given to you daily by my assistants.'

'Very well.'

'And consider this,' Kor said, hunching forward in his chair. 'Your failure with the Watchman made the Leader accuse me of failure. He will not tolerate excuses. If you fail the next time I call on you, it will be necessary to destroy you.'

'I understand perfectly.'

'Good. Return to your quarters until summoned. And remember, either we destroy Leoh, or he destroys us.'

Odal nodded, rose from his chair, and walked out of the office. *Us*, he thought. *Kor is beginning to feel the terror he uses on others.* If he could have been sure that he wasn't being watched by hidden cameras, Odal would have smiled.

*

Professor Leoh eased his bulky body into the softness of an air couch. It looked as though he was sitting on nothingness, with the glistening metal curve of the couch several centimeters from his body.

'This is what I've needed for a long time,' he said to Hector. 'A real vacation, with all the luxuries. It makes an old man happy.'

The Star Watchman was standing by the window wall across the room from Leoh, anxiously peering down at the bustling city far below. 'It's a nice apartment they've given you, all right.'

The room was long and spacious, with one whole side devoted to the window wall. The decorations were color- and scent-coded to change slowly through the day. At the moment the walls were in shades of brown and gold, and the air hinted faintly of spices.

'The best part of it,' Leoh said, stretching slowly on the couch, 'is that the dueling machine is fixed so that a telepath can't bring in outside helpers without setting off a warning alarm, and I've got nothing to do until the new school year begins at Carinae. I might not even go back then; as long as the Acquatainians want to treat me so royally, why shouldn't I spend a year or so here? There's plenty of research I can do ... perhaps even lecture occasionally at the university here ...'

Hector tried to smile at the old man's musings, but looked worried instead. 'Maybe you shouldn't stay in Acquatainia too long. I mean, well ... the Kerak people might still be after you. Odal was going to challenge you before I ... that is ...'

'Before you saved me.'

The Watchman's face colored. 'Well, I didn't really mean ... that is, it wasn't ...'

Leoh chuckled. 'Don't be so flustered, my boy. You're a hero. Surely Geri regards you as such.'

'Um, yes, I guess so.'

Changing the subject, Leoh asked, 'And how are your quarters? Comfortable, I hope.'

'Sure.' Hector nodded. 'The Terran embassy's almost as plush as this apartment.'

'Not bad for a junior lieutenant.'

Hector fidgeted from the window wall to the couch, then sat on the edge of a web chair.

'Are you nervous about Sir Harold's visit?' Leoh asked.

'N ... nervous? No, sir. Terrified!'

Laughing, Leoh said, 'Don't worry. Harold's a pleasant enough old grouse ... although he tries his best to hide it.'

Nodding without looking convinced, Hector got to his feet again and went back to the window wall. Then he gasped, 'He ... he's here!'

Leoh heaved himself up from the couch and hurried to see. A sleek ground car with Star Watch markings was pulled up at the building's entrance. Official Acquatainian escort cars flanked it.

'He must be on his way up,' Leoh said. 'Now try to relax and act ...'

The simple-minded door computer announced in a tinny monotone, 'Your expected guests are here.'

'Then open up,' Leoh commanded.

The door slid open to reveal a pair of sturdy, steel-eyed Watchmen, a half-dozen Acquatainian honor guards, and – in their midst – the paunchy, jowly figure of Sir Harold Spencer, dressed in a shapeless gray jump-suit.

The Star Watch Commander in Chief broke into one of his rare smiles. 'Albert, you old scoundrel, how are you?'

Leoh rushed to the doorway and grasped Spencer's outstretched hand. 'Harold ... I thought we'd never see each other again, in the flesh.'

'Considering the amount of flesh between the two of us, perhaps we're violating some basic law of the universe by being in the same room together.'

They laughed and walked into the room. The door slid shut, leaving the guards outside. Hector stood transfixed beside the window wall.

'Harold, you look wonderful ...'

'Nonsense. I'm a walking geriatrics experiment. But you, you ancient schemer, you must have transferred to another body since I saw you last.'

'No, merely careful living ...'

'Ahah. My downfall. Too many worries and too much wine. It must be pleasant to live the university life, free of care ...'

'Of course. Of course. Oh ... Harold, I'd like to introduce Junior Lieutenant Hector.'

Hector snapped to attention and saluted.

'Stand easy, Lieutenant. No need for formality. So, you're the man who beat Kerak's assassin, are you?'

'No, sir. I mean yessir ... I mean, Professor Leoh is the one ...'

'Nonsense. Albert told me all about it. You're the one who faced the danger.'

Hector's mouth twitched once or twice, as though he was trying to say something, but no sounds came out.

Spencer stuck a massive hand into his pocket and pulled out a small ebony box. 'This is for you, Lieutenant.' He handed the box to Hector.

The Watchman opened it and saw inside, against a jet-black setting, two small silver pins in the shape of comets. The insignia of a full lieutenant. His jaw dropped open.

'The official notification is grinding through Star Watch processing, Lieutenant,' Spencer said. 'I thought there was no sense letting you wait until the computers straightened out all the records. Congratulations on a well-earned promotion.'

Hector managed a half-strangled, 'Thank you, sir.'

Turning to Leoh, Spencer said, 'Now then, Albert, let us recount old times. I assume you have some refreshments on the premises?'

Several hours later the two old men were sitting on the air couch, while Hector listened from the web chair. The room's color had shifted to reds and yellows now, and the scent was of desert flowers.

'And what do you intend to do now?' Sir Harold was asking the Professor. 'Surely you don't expect me to believe that you're going to luxuriate here and then return to Carinae, in the midst of the deepest political crisis of the century.'

Leoh shrugged and hiked his eyebrows, an expression that sent a network of creases across his fleshy face. 'I'm not sure what I'm going to do. I'd still like to take a good look at some ideas for better interstellar transportation. And I'd want to be on hand here if those savages from Kerak try to use the dueling machine for their own purposes again.'

Nodding, Spencer rumbled, 'I knew it. You're getting yourself involved in politics. Sooner or later you'll be after my job.'

Even Hector laughed at that.

More seriously, Spencer went on, 'You know, of course, that I'm here officially to attend the inauguration of General Martine as the new Prime Minster.'

'Yes,' said Leoh. 'And your *real* reason for coming?'

Lowering his voice slightly, Spencer answered, 'I hope to persuade Martine to join the Commonwealth. Or at least to sign a treaty of alliance with us. It's the only way that Acquatainia can avoid a war with Kerak. All of Acquatainia's former allies have been taken over by Kerak or frightened off. Alone, the Acquatainians are in grave danger. As a Commonwealth member, or an ally, I doubt that even Kanus would be foolish enough to attack them right now.'

'But Acquatainia has always refused Commonwealth membership . . . or even an alliance.'

'Yes, but General Martine might see things differently now that Kanus is obviously preparing for war,' Spencer said.

'But the General . . .' Hector began, then stopped.

'Go on, my boy. What were you going to say?'

'Well, it might not be anything important . . . just something that Geri told me about the General . . . er, the Prime Minister. She, eh, well, she said he's a stubborn, shortsighted, proud old clod. Those were her words, sir.'

Spencer huffed. 'The Terran embassy here used slightly different terms, but they painted the same picture of him.'

'And, uh, she said he's also very brave and patriotic . . . but short-tempered.'

Leoh turned a worried expression toward Spencer. 'It doesn't sound as though he'd be willing to admit that he needs Commonwealth protection, does it?'

Shrugging, Sir Harold replied, 'The plain fact is that an alliance with the Commonwealth is the only way to avert a war. I've had our computer simulators study the situation. Now that Kerak has absorbed Szarno and has neutralized Acquatainia's other former allies, the computer predicts that Kerak will defeat Acquatainia in a war. Ninety-three per cent probability.'

Leoh's look of gloom sank deeper.

'And once Kanus has Acquatainia under his grasp, he'll attack the Commonwealth.'

'What? But that's suicide! Why should he do that?'

'I'd say it's because he's a lunatic,' Spencer answered, with real anger edging his voice. 'The sociodynamicists tell me that Kanus' sort of dictatorship must continually seek to expand, or it will fall apart from internal dissensions and pressures.'

'But he can't beat the Commonwealth,' Hector said.

'Correct,' Spencer agreed. 'Every computer simulation

we've run shows that the Commonwealth would crush Kerak, even if Kanus has Acquatainia's resources in his hands.'

The Star Watch Commander paused a moment, then added, 'But the computers also predict that the war will cost millions of lives on both sides. And it will trigger off other wars, elsewhere, that could eventually destroy the Commonwealth entirely.'

Leoh leaned back with the shock. 'Then – Martine simply *must* accept Commonwealth alliance.'

Spencer nodded. But his face showed that he didn't expect it.

*

Leoh and Hector watched General Martine's inauguration on tri-di, in the professor's apartment. That evening, they joined the throngs of politicians, businessmen, military leaders, ambassadors, artists, visitors, and other VIP's who were congregating at the city's main spaceport for the new Prime Minister's inaugural ball. The party was to be held aboard a satellite orbiting the planet.

'Do you think Geri will be there?' Hector asked Leoh as they pushed along with the crowd into a jammed shuttle craft.

The Watchman was wearing his dress black-and-silver uniform, with the comet insignias on his collar. Leoh wore a simple cover-all, as advised in the invitation to the party. It was a splendid crimson with gold trim.

'You said she's been invited,' Leoh answered over the hubbub of the hundreds of other conversations.

They found a pair of seats together and strapped themselves in.

'But she wasn't certain that she ought to go ... what with her father's death only a few weeks ago.'

Leaning back in the padded chair, Leoh said, 'Well, if she's not there, you can spend hours telling her all about the party.'

86

The Watchman's lean face broke into a toothy grin. 'I hadn't thought of that . . .'

The shuttle filled quickly with noisy party goers and then took off. It flew like a normal rocket plane to the top of the atmosphere, then boosted swiftly to the satellite. The party was well under way when Hector and Leoh stepped from the shuttle's air lock into the satellite.

It was a huge globular satellite, with all the interior decks and bulkheads removed so that it was as hollow as an enormous soap bubble. The shell of the 'bubble' was transparent, except for small disks around the various air locks.

There must have been more than a thousand people present already, Leoh guessed as he took a first look at the milling throng floating weightlessly through the vast globe. They seemed to be suspended over his head, many of them upside down, others hanging sideways or calmly drifting along and gesturing, deep in conversation. Most of them held drinks in sealed plastic squeeze containers with straws poking out from their tops. The crowd formed a dizzying kaleidoscope overhead: brilliant costumes, flashing jewelry, buzzing voices, crackling laughter, all mixing and gliding effortlessly in midair.

Leoh put a hand out to Hector, to steady himself.

'Must be some sort of grav field along the shell,' the Watchman said, pulling one boot tackily from the floor.

'For the fainthearted, I suppose,' Leoh said.

The other shuttle passengers were streaming past them and launching themselves like swimmers away from the air lock, coasting gracefully up into the huge chamber.

Looking around, Leoh saw refreshment bars spotted along the shell, and more floating overhead. He turned back to Hector and said, 'Why don't you go look for Geri, and I'll try to find Harold.'

'I sort of think I should stay close to you, Professor. After all, my job is to, uh, that is . . .'

'Nonsense! There are no Kerak assassins in this crowd. Go find Geri.'

Grinning, Hector said, 'All right. But I'll be keeping one eye on you.'

With that, Hector jumped off the floor to join the weightless throng. But he jumped a bit too hard, banged into a rainbow-clad Acquatainian who was floating past with a drink in his hand, and knocked the drink, the man, and himself spinning. The drink's cover popped open and globules of liquid spattered through the air, hitting other members of the crowd and breaking into constantly smaller droplets. A woman screamed.

The Acquatainian righted himself immediately, but Hector couldn't stop. He went tumbling head over heels, cleaving through the crowd like a runaway chariot, emitting a string of, 'Wh . . . whoops . . . look out . . . gosh . . . pardon me . . . watch it . . .'

Leoh stood rooted to his spot beside the air lock, staring unbelievingly as Hector barreled through the crowd. The weightless guests scattered before him, some yelling angrily, a few women screaming, most of them laughing. Then they closed in again, and Leoh could no longer see the Watchman. A trio of servants took off after him, chasing across the gigantic globe to intercept him.

Only then did Leoh notice a servant standing beside him, with a slim belt in his hands. 'A stabilizer, sir. Most of the guests have their own. It is very difficult to maneuver weightlessly without one . . . as the Star Watchman is demonstrating.'

Leoh accepted the belt, decided there wasn't much he could do about Hector except add to the confusion, so he floated easily up into the heart of the party. The sensation of weightlessness was pleasant, like floating in a pool of water. He got himself a drink in one of the special covered cups and sucked on the straw as he drifted toward a large knot of people near the center of the globe.

Suddenly Hector pinwheeled past him, looking helpless and red-faced, as a couple of servants swam after him as hard as they could. The party goers laughed as Hector buzzed by, then returned to their conversations. Leoh put out a hand, but the Watchman was past and disappeared into the crowd again.

Leoh frowned. He loathed big parties. Too many people, too little activity. People talked incessantly at parties, but said nothing. They ate and drank despite the fact that they weren't hungry. They spent hours listening to total strangers whom they would never see again. It was a mammoth waste of time.

Or are you merely bored, he asked himself, *because no one here recognizes you? They seem to be having a fine time without the famous inventor of the dueling machine.*

Leoh drifted toward the transparent wall of the satellite and watched the glowing surface of the planet outside, a huge solid sphere bathed in golden sunlight. Then he turned and floated effortlessly until he got a good view of the stars. The Acquataine Cluster was a jewel box of gleaming red and gold and orange stars, packed together so thickly that you could barely see the black background of space.

So much beauty in the universe, Leoh thought.

'Professor Leoh?'

Startled out of his reverie, Leoh turned to see a small, moon-faced, balding man floating beside him and extending his hand in greeting.

'I am Lal Ponte,' he said as Leoh shook his hand. 'It is an honor to meet you.'

'An honor for me,' Leoh replied with the standard Acquatainian formality.

'You are probably looking for Sir Harold, and I know the Prime Minister would like to see you. Since they're both in the same place, may I take you to them?' Ponte's voice was a squeaky tenor.

Leoh nodded. 'Thanks. Lead the way.'

Ponte took off across the satellite, worming his way around knots of people – many of them upside down. Leoh followed. *Like a freighter being towed by a tug,* he thought of the sight of his bulky self tagging along after the mousy-looking Acquatainian.

Leoh searched his memory. Lal Ponte: the new Secretary of Interior Affairs. Until a few weeks ago, Ponte had been an insignificant member of the legislature. But in the hectic voting for a new Prime Minister, with four possible candidates splitting the legislature almost evenly, Ponte had risen from obscurity to bring a critical dozen votes to General Martine's side. His reward was the Cabinet position.

Ponte glided straight into an immense clot of people near the very center of the satellite. Leoh followed him ponderously, bumping shoulders and elbows, getting frowns and mutterings, apologizing like a latecomer to the theater who must step on many toes to reach his seat.

'Who's the old one?' he heard a feminine voice whisper.

'Ah, Albert, there you are!' Spencer called as they got to the center of the crowd. With that, the crowd flowed back slightly to make room for Leoh. The mutterings took on a different tone.

'General Martine,' Spencer said to the new Prime Minister, 'you of course know Albert Leoh, the inventor of the dueling machine and one of the Commonwealth's leading scientists.'

A buzz of recognition went through the crowd.

Martine was tall and slim, wearing a military uniform of white and gold that accentuated his lean frame. His face was long, serious, with sad hound's eyes and a prominent patrician nose. He nodded and put on a measured smile. 'Of course. The man who defeated Kerak's assassin. It is good to see you again, Professor.'

'Thank you for inviting me,' Leoh responded. 'And congratulations on your election.'

Martine nodded gravely.

'I have been trying to convince the Prime Minister,'

Spencer said in his heavy public-address voice, 'that Acquatainia would benefit greatly from joining the Commonwealth, to win the war, once it begins.'

Martine raised his eyes to look beyond the crowd, out toward the satellite's transparent shell and the golden planet beyond.

'Acquatainia has traditionally remained independent of the Commonwealth,' Martine said. 'We have no need of special trade advantages or political alliances. We are a rich and strong and happy people.'

'But you are threatened by Kerak,' Leoh said.

'My dear Professor,' Martine said, raising himself slightly and looking down on Leoh, 'I have been a military man all my adult life. I had the honor of helping to defeat Kerak a generation ago. I know how to deal with military threats.'

Far across the satellite, at one of the air lock entrances, Hector – wearing a stabilizer belt now – hovered above a crowd of latecomers as they came through the air lock, searching their faces. And there she was!

He rushed down into them, accidentally pushing three jeweled and cloaked businessmen into an equal number of mini-gowned wives, stepping on the foot of a burly Acquatainian colonel, and jostling through the new arrivals to get to Geri Dulaq.

'You came,' he said, taking both her hands in his.

Her smile made his knees flutter. 'I hoped you'd be here, Hector.'

'I ... well,' he was grinning like an idiot, 'I'm here.'

'I'm glad.'

They stood there at the air lock entrance, looking at each other, while people elbowed their way around them to get into the party.

'Hector, shouldn't we move away from the air lock?' Geri suggested gently.

'Huh? Oh, sure ...' He walked her toward a slightly

sweaty servant (one of the posse who had chased Hector across the satellite) and then took a stabilizer belt from him.

'You'll need one of these belts before you try to float. Otherwise it's, eh, kind of tricky trying to maneuver.'

The servant gritted his teeth and glared.

Geri blinked her large brown eyes at Hector. 'Will you show me how it works? I'm terribly poor at things like this.'

Restraining an impulse to leap off the floor and do a triple somersault, Hector said simply, 'Oh, there's really nothing to it ...' he glanced at the sweaty-faced servant, then added, 'once you get the hang of it.'

Spencer was saying, with some edge to his voice, 'But when you defeated Kerak, you had the Szarno Confederacy and several other star-nations on your side. Now your old alliances are gone. You are alone against Kerak.'

Martine sighed like a man being forced to exert great patience. 'I repeat, Sir Harold, that Acquatainia is strong enough to defeat any Kerak attack without Star Watch assistance.'

Leoh shook his head, but said nothing.

Lal Ponte, floating beside his Prime Minister and looking like a small satellite near a large planet, said, 'The Prime Minister is making plans for an impenetrable defense system, a network of fortified planets and star-ship fleets so strong that Kerak would never dare to attack it.'

'And suppose,' Spencer countered, 'Kerak attacks before this defense line is completed? Or attacks from a different direction?'

'We will fight and win,' Martine said.

Spencer ran a hand through his shaggy hair. 'Don't you realize that an alliance with the Commonwealth – even a token alliance – will force Kanus to pause before he dares to attack? Your objective, it seems to me, should be to prevent a war from starting. Instead, you're concentrating on plans to win the war, once it begins.'

'If Kanus wants war,' Martine said, 'we will defeat him.'

'But he can be defeated without war,' Spencer insisted.

Leoh added, 'No dictator can last long without the threat of war to keep his people frightened enough to serve him. And if it becomes clear that Acquatainia cannot be attacked successfully . . .'

'Kanus wants war,' Martine said.

'And so do you, apparently,' Spencer added.

The Prime Minister glared at Spencer for a long moment, then turned and said, 'Excuse me, I am neglecting my other guests.'

He pushed away, accompanied by a half-dozen followers, leaving Spencer, Leoh, and Lal Ponte in the middle of a suddenly dissipating crowd.

Geri and Hector floated close to the transparent shell, looking out at the stars, barely aware of the music and voices from the party.

'Hector.'

'Yes?'

'Will you promise me something?'

'Sure. What is it?'

Her face was so serious, so beautiful, he could feel his pulse throbbing through his body.

'Do you think Odal will ever return to Acquatainia?'

The question surprised him. 'Uh . . . I don't know. Maybe. I sort of doubt it. I mean, well . . .'

'If he ever does . . .' Geri's voice trailed off.

'Don't worry,' Hector said, holding her close to him. 'I won't let him hurt you . . . or anybody else.'

Her smile was overpowering. 'Hector, dearest Hector. If Odal should ever return here, would you kill him for me?'

Without a microsecond's thought, he replied, 'I'd challenge him as soon as I saw him.'

Her face grew serious again. 'No. I don't mean in the dueling machine. I mean really. Kill him.'

'I don't understand the Prime Minister's attitude,' Leoh said to Spencer and Lal Ponte.

'He has great pride,' Ponte answered, 'the pride of a military man. And we have great pride in him. He is the man who can lead Acquatainia back to glory. Dulaq and Massan ... they were good men, but civilians, too weak to deal with Kanus of Kerak.'

'They were political leaders,' Spencer rumbled. 'They realized that war is an admission of failure. War is the last resort, when all else fails.'

'We are not afraid of war!' Ponte snapped.

'You should be,' Leoh said.

'Why? Do you doubt that we could defeat Kerak?'

'Why run the risk when you could avoid the war altogether?'

The little politician waved his arms agitatedly, a maneuver that caused him to bob up and down weightlessly. 'We are not afraid of the Kerak Worlds! You assume that we are cowards who must run under the skirts of your Terran Commonwealth at the first sign of danger!'

'Lack of judgment is worse than cowardice,' said Leoh. 'Why do you insist? ...'

'You accuse the Acquatainian government of stupidity?'

'No, I ...'

His voice rising higher and higher, Ponte squeaked, 'Then you accuse me of stupidity ... or the Prime Minister, perhaps?'

'I am only questioning your judgment about ...'

'And I accuse you of cowardice!' Ponte screeched.

People were turning to watch them now. Ponte bobbed up and down, raging. 'Because *you* are afraid of this bully, Kanus, you assume that we should be!'

'Now really ...' Spencer began.

'You are a coward!' Ponte screamed at Leoh. 'And I will prove it. I challenge you to meet me in your own dueling machine!'

For the first time in years, Leoh felt his own temper flaring. 'This is the most asinine argument I've ever seen.'

'I challenge you!' Ponte insisted. 'Do you accept the challenge, or will you slink away and prove your cowardice?'

'Accepted!' Leoh snapped.

*

The sun was a small bluish-white disk high in the sky of Meklin, one of Kerak's forced agriculture planets. Up here on the ridge, the wind felt chill to Odal, despite the heat in the valley farmlands below. The sky was cloudless, but the wind-rippled trees rustled a mosaic of gold and red against the blue.

Odal saw Runstet sitting on the grass in a patch of sunlight with his wife and three small children. The oldest, a boy, could hardly have been more than ten. They were enjoying a picnic, laughing at something that had escaped Odal's notice.

The Kerak major stepped forward. Runstet saw him and paled. He got up to face Odal.

'This is not what I want to see,' Odal said quietly. 'You'll have to do better.'

Runstet stood there, rooted to the spot, while everything around him began to flicker, dim. The children and their mother, still laughing, grew faint and their laughter faded. The woods seemed to go misty, then disappeared altogether. Nothing was visible except Runstet and the fearful look on his face.

'You are trying to hide your memories from me by substituting other memories,' Odal said. 'We know that you met with certain other high-ranking army officers at your home three months ago. You claim it was a social occasion. I would like to see it.'

The older man, square-jawed, his hair an iron gray, was obviously fighting for self-control. Fear was in him, Odal knew, but he also sensed something else: anger, stubbornness, and pride.

'Inferior-grade officers were not invited to the ... to the party. It was strictly for my old classmates, Major.' General Runstet accented the last word with as much venom as he could muster.

Odal felt a flash of anger, but replied calmly, 'May I remind you that you are under arrest and therefore have no rank. And if you insist on refusing me access to your memories of this meeting, more stringent methods of interrogation will be used.' *Fool!* he thought. *You're a dead man and yet you refuse to admit it.*

'You can do anything you want to,' Runstet said. 'Drugs, torture ... you'll get nothing from me. Use this damnable dueling machine for a hundred years and I'll still tell you nothing!'

Unmoving, Odal said, 'Shall I recreate the scene for you? I have visited your home in Meklin, and I have a list of the officers who attended your meeting.'

'When Marshal Lugal learns how Kor and his trained assassins have treated a general officer, you'll all be exterminated!' Runstet bellowed. 'And you! An officer yourself. A disgrace to the uniform you wear!'

'I have my duty,' Odal said. 'And I am trying to spare you some of the more unpleasant methods of interrogation.'

As Odal spoke, the mist around them dissolved and they were standing in a spacious living-room. Sunlight streamed through the open patio doors. Nearly a dozen men in army uniforms sat on the couches. But they were silent, unmoving.

'Now then,' said Odal, 'you will show me exactly what happened. Every word and gesture, every facial expression.'

'Never!'

'That in itself is an admission of guilt,' Odal snapped. 'You have been plotting against the Leader; you and a number of others of the general staff.'

'I will not incriminate other men,' Runstet said stubbornly. 'You can kill me, but . . .'

'We can kill your wife and children, too,' Odal said softly.

The General's mouth popped open and Odal could feel the panic flash through him. 'You wouldn't dare! Not even Kanus himself would . . .'

'Accidents happen,' said Odal. 'As far as the rest of Kerak is concerned you are hospitalized with a mental breakdown. Your despondent wife might take her own life, or your entire family could die in a crash while on their way to the hospital to see you.'

Runstet seemed to crumple. He did not physically move or say a word, but his entire body seemed to soften, to sag. Behind him, one of the generals stirred to life. He leaned forward, took a cigar from the humidor on the low table before him, and said:

'When we're ready to attack the Acquatainians, just how far can we trust Kanus to allow the army to operate without political interference?'

*

'I simply don't understand what came over me,' Leoh said to Spencer and Hector. 'I never let my temper get the better of me.'

They were standing in the former lecture hall that housed the grotesque bulk of the dueling machine. No one else had entered yet; the duel with Ponte was still an hour away.

'Come now, Albert,' said Spencer. 'If that whining little politician had spoken to me the way he did to you, I'd have been tempted to hit him there and then.'

Leoh shrugged.

'These Acquatanians are an emotional lot,' Spencer went on. 'Frankly, I'm glad to be leaving.'

'When will you go?'

'As soon as this silly duel is finished. It's quite clear that Martine is unwilling to accept any support from the Commonwealth. My presence here is merely aggravating him and his people.'

Hector spoke for the first time. 'That means there'll be war between Acquatainia and Kerak.' He said it quietly, his eyes gazing off into space, as though he were talking to himself.

'Both sides want war,' Spencer said.

'Stupidity,' muttered Leoh.

'Pride,' Spencer corrected. 'The same kind of pride that makes men fight duels.'

Startled, Leoh was about to answer until he saw the grin on Spencer's leathery face.

The chamber filled slowly. The meditechs who operated the dueling machine came in, a few at a time and started checking out the machine. There was a new man on the team, sitting at a new console. His equipment monitored the duels and made certain that neither of the duelists was getting telepathic help from outside.

Ponte and his group arrived precisely at the appointed time for the duel. Four newsmen appeared in the press gallery, high above. Leoh suppressed a frown. *Surely a duel involving the machine's inventor should warrant more attention from the networks.*

They went through the medical checks, the instructions on using the machine (which Leoh had written), and the agreement that the challenged party would have the first choice of weapons.

'My weapon will be the elementary laws of physics,' Leoh said. 'No special intructions will be necessary.'

Ponte's eyes widened slightly with puzzlement. His seconds glanced at each other. Even the dueling machine's meditechs looked uncertain. After a heartbeat's silence, the chief meditech shrugged.

'If there are no objections,' he said, 'let us proceed.'

Leoh sat patiently in his booth while the meditechs attached the neurocontacts to his head and torso. *Strange, he* thought. *I've operated dueling machines hundreds of times. But this is the first time the other man in the machine is really angry at me. He wants to kill me.*

The meditechs left and shut the booth. Leoh was alone now, staring into the screen and its subtly shifting colors. He tried to close his eyes, found that he couldn't, tried again and succeeded.

When he opened them he was standing in the middle of a large, gymnasium-like room. There were windows high up near the lofty ceiling. Instead of being filled with athletic apparatus, this room was crammed with rope pulleys, inclined ramps, metal spheres of all sizes from a few centimeters to twice the height of a man. Leoh was standing on a slightly raised, circular platform, holding a small control box in his hand.

Lal Ponte stood across the room, his back to a wall, frowning at the jungle of unfamiliar equipment.

'This is a sort of elementary physics lab,' Leoh called out to him. 'While none of the objects here are really weapons, many of them can be dangerous if you know how to use them. Or if you don't know.'

Ponte began to object, 'This is unreasonable . . .'

'Not really,' Leoh said pleasantly. 'You'll find that the equipment is spread around the room to form a sort of maze. Your job is to get through the maze to this platform, and to find something to use as a weapon on me. Now, there are traps in the maze. You'll have to avoid them. And this platform is really a turntable . . . but we'll talk about that later.'

Ponte looked around. 'You are foolish.'

'Perhaps.'

The Acquatainian took a few steps to his right and lifted a slender metal rod. Hefting it in his hand, he started toward Leoh.

'That's a lever,' the Professor said. 'Of course, you can use it as a club if you wish.'

99

A tangle of ropes stood in Ponte's way. Instead of detouring around them, he pushed his way through.

Leoh shook his head and touched a button on his control box. 'A mistake, I'm afraid.'

The ropes – a pulley, actually – jerked into motion and heaved the flooring under Ponte's feet upward. The Acquatainian toppled to his hands and knees and found himself on a platform suddenly ten meters in the air. Dropping the lever, he began grabbing at the ropes. One of them swung free and he jumped at it, curling his arms and legs around it.

'Pendulum,' Leoh called to him. 'Watch your . . .'

Ponte's rope, with him on it, swung out a little way, then swung back again toward the mid-air platform. He cracked his head nastily on the platform's edge, let go of the rope, and thudded to the floor.

'The floor's padded,' Leoh said, 'but I forgot to pad the edge of the platform. Hope it didn't hurt you too badly.'

Ponte sat up groggily, his head rolling. It took him three tries to stand up again. He staggered forward.

'On your right is an inclined plane of the sort Galileo used, only much larger. You'll have to hurry to get past the ball . . .'

At a touch of Leoh's finger on the control box, an immense metal ball began rolling down the gangway-sized plane. Ponte heard its rumbling, turned to stare at it goggle-eyed, and barely managed to jump out of its way. The ball rolled across the floor, ponderously smashing everything in its way until it crashed against the far wall.

'Perhaps you'd better sit down for a few moments and gather your wits,' Leoh suggested.

Ponte was puffing hard. 'You . . . you're a devil . . . a smiling devil.'

He reached down for a small sphere at his feet. As he raised his hand to throw it, Leoh touched the control box again and the turntable platform began to rotate slowly. Ponte's awkward toss missed him by a meter.

'I can adjust the turntable's speed,' Leoh explained as Ponte threw several more spheres. All missed.

The Acquatainian, his once-bland face furiously red now, rushed toward the spinning platform and jumped onto it, on the side opposite Leoh. He still had two small spheres in his hand.

'Be careful,' Leoh warned as Ponte swayed and nearly fell off. 'Centrifugal force can be tricky . . .'

The two men stood unmoving for a moment: Leo alertly watching, Ponte glaring. The room appeared to be swinging around them.

Ponte threw one of the spheres as hard as he could. It seemed to curve away from Leoh.

'The Coriolis force,' said Leoh, in a slightly lecturing tone, 'is a natural phenomenon on rotating systems. It's what makes the winds curve across a planet's rotating surface.'

The second sphere whistled by, no closer than the first.

'I should also warn you that this platfrom is made of alternate sections of magnetic and nonmagnetic materials.' Leoh gestured toward the mosaic-colored floor. 'Your shoes have metal in them. If you remain on the magnetized sections, the red ones, you should be able to move about without too much difficulty.'

He touched the control box again and the turntable speeded up considerably. The room seemed to whirl wildly around them now. Leoh hunched down and leaned inward.

'Of course,' he went on, 'at the speed we're going now, if you should step onto a nonmagnetized section . . .'

Ponte started doggedly across the turntable, heading for Leoh, his eyes on the colored flooring. Leoh stepped carefully away from him, keeping as much distance between them as possible. Ponte was moving faster now, trying to keep one eye on Leoh and one on his feet. He stopped abruptly, started to move directly toward Leoh, cutting in toward the center of the turntable.

'Be careful!'

Ponte's feet slipped out from under him. He fell painfully on his back, skidded across the turntable out to the edge, and shot across the floor to slam feet first into a big metal block.

'My leg . . .' He groaned. 'My leg is broken . . .'

Leoh stopped the turntable and stepped off. He walked over to the Acquatainian, whose face was twisted wih pain.

'I could kill you fairly easily now,' he said softly. 'But I really have no desire to. You've had enough, I think.'

The room began to fade out. Leoh found himself sitting in the dueling machine's booth, blinking at the now dead screen in front of him.

The door popped open and Hector's grinning face appeared. 'You beat him !'

'Yes,' Leoh said suddenly tired. 'But I didn't kill him. He can try again with his own choice of weapons, if he chooses to.'

Ponte was white-faced and trembling as they walked toward him. His followers were huddled around him, asking questions. The chief meditech was saying :

'You may continue, if you wish, or postpone the second half of the duel until tomorrow.'

Looking up at Leoh, Ponte shook his head. 'No . . . no. I was defeated. I can't . . . fight again.'

The chief meditech nodded. 'The duel is concluded, then. Professor Leoh has won.'

Leoh extended his hand to the Acquatainian. Ponte's grasp was soft and sweaty.

'I hope we can be friends now,' Leoh said.

Looking thoroughly miserable, Ponte mumbled, 'Yes, of course. Thank you.'

*

Long after everyone else had left the dueling machine chamber, Leoh, Spencer, and Hector remained behind, pacing slowly across the tiled floor, speaking in low voices that echoed gloomily in the vast room.

'I must go now, Albert,' Spencer said. 'My ship was scheduled to leave half an hour ago. My adjutant, outside, is probably eating tranquilizers by now. He's a good man, but extremely nervous.'

'And there's nothing you can do to convince Martine?' Leoh asked.

'Apparently not. But if you're going to remain on the scene here, perhaps you can try.'

Leoh nodded. 'I can speak to the scientists here at the university. Their voices should carry some weight with the government.'

Spencer looked skeptical. 'What else will you be tinkering with? I know you won't be content without some sort of research problem to puzzle over.'

'I'm trying to find a way of improving on the star ships. We've got to make interstellar travel easier ...'

'The star ships are highly efficient already.'

'I know. I mean a fundamental improvement. Perhaps a completely different way to travel through space ... as different as the star ships are from the ancient rockets.'

Spencer held up a beefy hand. 'Enough! In another minute you'll start spouting metadimensional physics at me. Politics is hard enough for me to understand.'

Leoh chuckled.

Turning to Hector, Sir Harold said, 'Lieutenant, keep a close eye on him as long as he's in Acquatainia. Professor Leoh is a valuable man – and my friend. Understood?'

'Yessir.'

*

Odal stood rigidly at attention before Kor. The Intelligence Minister was leaning back in his padded desk chair, his hands playing over an ornate dagger that he used as a pointer.

'You don't enjoy your duties here?' Kor was smiling coldly.

'I am an army officer,' Odal said carefully. 'I find that interrogation work is ... unpleasant.'

Kor tapped the dagger against his fingernails. 'But you are

103

one of the few men who can use the dueling machine for interrogation. And you are by far the best man we have for the purpose. The others are amateurs compared to you. You have talent!'

'It is difficult for me to interrogate fellow army officers.'

'I suppose so,' Kor admitted. 'But you have done quite well. We now know exactly who in the army we can trust, and who is plotting against the Leader.'

'Then my work here is finished.'

'The plotting involves more than the army, Major. It goes far wider and deeper. The enemies of the Leader infest every part of our government. Marshal Lugal is involved, I'm sure . . .'

'But there's no evidence . . .'

'I'm convinced he's involved,' Kor snapped. 'And Romis, too!'

Kanus wants control of the army, Odal knew, and you want to eliminate anyone who can compete with you for Kanus' favor.

'Don't look so sour, Major,' said Kor, his smile broader and somehow more chilling. 'You have served your Leader – and me – very well in these weeks. Now then . . . how would you like to return to Acquatainia?'

Odal felt a shock of surprise and strange elation.

'Spencer has left Acquatainia,' Kor explained, 'and our plans are going well. But Leoh still remains there. He is still dangerous. You will destroy him.'

'And the Watchman too,' Odal said.

Kor jabbed the dagger toward Odal. 'Not so fast. Leoh will be destroyed by his own dueling machine, but in a very special way. In fact, he has already taken the first step toward his own destruction, in a duel with a simple little man who thinks he will be Prime Minister of Acquatainia, once Kerak conquers the Cluster.'

Frowning, Odal said, 'I don't understand.'

'You will, Major. You probably won't enjoy what you

must do, any more than Lal Ponte did. But you will do your duty to Kerak and to the Leader, just as Ponte did what we told him to. You won't become Prime Minister of Acquatainia, of course – but then, neither will Lal Ponte.'

Kor's laugh was like a knife scraping on bone.

*

The night sky of Acquatainia was a blaze of stars twinkling, shimmering, dazzling so brightly that there was no real darkness in the city, only a silvery twilight brighter than full moonlight on Earth.

Hector sat at the controls of the skimmer and raced it down the river that cut through the city, heading toward the harbor and the open ocean. He could smell the salt air already. He glanced across the skimmer's tiny cockpit at Geri, sitting in the swivel seat beside him and hunched slightly forward to keep the spray off her face. The sight of her almost made it impossible for him to concentrate on steering the high-speed skimmer.

He snaked the little vessel through the other pleasure boats on the river, trailing a plume of slightly luminous spray. Out in the harbor there were huge freighters anchored massively in the main channel. Hector ran the skimmer over to shallower water, between the channel and the docks as Geri stared up at the vast ocean-going ships.

Finally they were out on the deep swells of the sea. Hector cut the engine and the skimmer slowed, dug its prow into an oncoming billow, and settled its hull in the water.

'The rocking isn't going to . . . uh, bother you, is it?' he asked, turning to Geri.

Shaking her head, she said, 'Oh no, I love it here on the sea.' Now that they were resting easily on the water, Geri reached up and unpinned her hair. It fell around her shoulders with a softness that made Hector quiver.

'The cooker should be finished by now,' she said. 'Are you hungry?'

He nodded. They got up together, bumped slightly as they squeezed between the two swivel seats to get to the padded bench at the rear of the cockpit. Geri smiled at him and Hector plopped back in the pilot's seat, content to savor her perfume and watch her. She sat on the bench and opened the cooker's hatch. Out came steaming trays of food.

Hector came over to the bench, stumbling slightly, and sat beside her.

'The drinks are in the cooler,' she said, pointing to the other side of the bench.

After dinner they sat together on the bench, heads back to gaze at the stars, while the skimmer's autopilot kept them from drifting too far from the harbor.

'This, uh . . . thing about Odal,' Hector said, very reluctantly. 'It's not . . . well, it's not the kind of thing that . . .'

'I know. It's a terrible thing to ask you to do.' She put her hand in his. 'But what else can I do? I'm only a girl; I can't go out and kill him myself. I need a protector, a champion, someone who will avenge my father's murder. You're the only one I can turn to, Hector.'

'Yes, but . . . um . . . killing him, that's . . .'

'It'll be dangerous, I realize that. But you're so brave. You're not afraid of Odal, are you?'

'No, but . . .'

'And it won't be anything more than a justifiable execution. He's a murderer. You'll be the sword of justice. My sword of justice.'

'Yes, but . . .'

She pulled away slightly. 'Of course, Odal will probably never return to Acquatainia. But if he does, you can be sure it's for one thing only.'

Hector blinked. 'What's that?'

'To murder Professor Leoh,' she said.

The Star Watchman slumped back on the bench. 'You're right. And I guess I've got to stop him from doing that.'

Geri turned and grabbed him by the ears and kissed him.

Hector felt his feet come off the deck. He held onto her and kissed back. Then she slid away from him. He reached for her, but she took his hand in hers.

'Let me catch my breath,' she said.

He eased over toward her, feeling his heart thumping louder than the slap of the waves against the skimmer's hull.

'Of course,' Geri said coolly, 'it seems that Professor Leoh can take care of himself in the dueling machine.'

'Uh-huh.' Hector edged closer to her.

'It was very surprising to hear that Lal Ponte had challenged the Professor,' she said, backing into the corner of the bench. 'Ponte is such a . . . a *nothing* type of person. I never thought he'd have the courage to fight a duel.'

Leaning close to Geri and sliding an arm across the bench's backrest and around her shoulders, Hector said nothing.

'I remember my father saying that if anyone in the legislature was working for Kerak, it would be Ponte.'

'Huh?'

Geri was frowning with the memory. 'Yes, Father was concerned that Ponte was allied with Kerak. "If Kerak ever conquers us," Father said to me once, "that little coward will be our Prime Minister."'

Hector sat upright. 'But now he's serving Martine . . . and Martine sure isn't pro-Kerak.'

'I know,' Geri said, nodding. 'Perhaps Father was wrong. Or Ponte may have changed his mind. Or . . .'

'Or he could still be working for Kerak.'

Geri smiled. 'Even if he is, Professor Leoh took care of him.'

'Umm.' Hector leaned back again and saw that he and Geri had somehow moved slightly apart. He pushed over toward her.

'My foot!' Geri leaped up from the bench.

'Oh, I'm sorry. Did I step on . . .' Hector jumped up too.

Geri was hopping on one foot in the tiny cockpit, making the skimmer rock with each bounce. Hector reached out to hold her, but she pushed him away. The effort toppled her over backward. The cockpit gunwale caught her behind the knees and she flipped backward, howling, into the water with a good-sized splash.

Hector, appalled, never hesitated a second. He leaped right into the sea from the point where he stood, narrowly missing Geri as he hit the water, head first, arms and legs flailing.

He came up spouting, blurry-eyed, gasping. Geri was treading water beside him.

'I . . . I . . . I . . .'

She laughed. 'It's all right, Hector. It's my own fault. I lost my temper when you stepped on my foot.'

'But . . . I . . . are you? . . .'

'It's a lovely night,' she said. 'As long as we're in the water anyway, why don't we have a swim?'

'Uh . . . fine, except, well, that is . . . I can't swim,' Hector said, and slowly he sank under.

*

As he stepped from the ramp of the spaceship to the slideway that led into the terminal building, Odal felt a strange sense of exhilaration.

He was in Acquatainia again! The warm sunlight, the bustling throngs of people, the gleaming towers of the city – he almost felt Dulaq's sense of joy about being here. Of course, Odal told himself, it's probably just a reaction to being free of Kor's dreary Ministry of Intelligence. But the Kerak major had to admit to himself – as he moved toward the spaceport terminal, escorted by four of Kor's men – that Acquatainia had a rhythm, a freshness, a sense of freedom and gaiety that he had never found on Kerak.

Inside the terminal building, he had fifty meters of automated inspectors to walk through before he could get into the ground car that would take him to the Kerak embassy. If there was going to be trouble, it would be here.

Two of his escorts got into the inspection line ahead of him, two behind.

Odal walked slowly between the two full-length X-ray screens and then stopped before the radiation detector. He inserted his passport and embassy identification cards into the correct slot in the computer's registration processor.

Then he heard someone in the next line, a woman's voice, saying, 'It is him! I recognize the uniform from the tri-di news.'

'Couldn't be,' a man's voice answered. 'They wouldn't dare send him back here.'

Odal purposely turned their way and smiled gravely at them. The woman said, 'I *told* you it was him!' Her husband glared at Odal.

Kor had arranged for a few newsmen to be on hand. As Odal collected his cards and travel kit at the end of the inspection line, a small knot of cameramen began grinding their tapers at him. He walked briskly toward the nearest doors, and the ground car that he could see waiting outside. His four escorts kept the newsmen at arm's length.

'Major Odal, don't you consider it risky to return to Acquatainia?'

'Do you think diplomatic immunity covers assassination?'

'Aren't you afraid someone might take a shot at you?'

The newsmen yelped after him like a pack of puppies following a man with an armful of bones. But Odal could feel the hatred now. Not so much from the newsmen, but from the rest of the people in the crowded terminal lobby. They stared at him, hating him. Before, when he was Kerak's invincible warrior, they feared him, even envied him. But now there was nothing in the crowd but hatred for the Kerak major, Odal knew.

He ducked into the ground car and sank into the back seat. Kor's guards filled the rest of the car. The door slammed shut, and some of the emotion and noise coming from the terminal crowd was cut off. For the first time, Odal thought about why he had returned to Acquatainia. Leoh. He frowned at the thought of what he had to do. But when he thought about Hector, about revenging himself for the Star Watchman's absurd victory in their duel, he allowed himself to smile.

*

Leoh sat slumped at the desk chair in the office behind the dueling machine chamber. He had some thinking to do, and his apartment was too comfortable for creative thought.

Through the closed door of the office he heard an outer door bang, hard fast-moving footsteps and a piercing off-key whistle. With a reluctant smile, he told the door-control to open. Hector was standing there with a fist raised, ready to knock.

'How'd you know?...'

'I'm partly telepathic,' Leoh said.

'Really? I didn't know. Do you think that helped you in your duel with ... oh, that's what I wanted to talk to you about ...'

Leoh raised a hand for silence. 'Come in, my boy, and sit down. Tell me, have you seen the tri-di newscasts this morning?'

Taking a chair next to the Professor, Hector said, 'No, sir, I, uh, got in kind of late last night and sort of late getting up this morning ... Got some water in my left ear ... it gurgles every time I move my head ...'

With an effort, Leoh stayed on the subject. 'The newscasts showed Odal landing at the main spaceport. He's returned.'

Hector jerked as though someone had stuck him with a pin. 'He ... he's back?'

'Now don't get rattled,' Leoh said as calmly as he could.

'No one's going to come in here with pistols blazing to assassinate me.'

'Maybe ... but, well, I mean ... there's a chance that Odal – or somebody – will try something.'

'Nonsense,' Leoh grumbled.

Hector didn't reply. He seemed to be lost in an inner debate; his face was flashing through a series of expressions: worried, puzzled, determined.

'What's the matter?' Leoh asked.

'Huh? Oh, nothing . . . just thinking.'

'This news about Odal has upset you more than I thought it would.'

'No, no . . . I'm not upset . . . just, uh, thinking.' Hector shook his head, as if trying to clear his mind. Leoh thought he could hear the gurgling of water.

'It's my duty,' Hector said, 'to, uh, protect you. So I'll have to stay, well, very close to you at all times. I think I should move into your apartment and stay with you wherever you go.'

Now Leoh found himself upset more than he thought he would be. But he knew that if he didn't let the Watchman stay close to him openly, Hector would try to do it secretly, which would merely be more agonizing for both of them.

'All right, my boy, if you insist; although I think you're being overly dramatic about this.'

Hector said, 'No, I've got to be there when Odal shows up . . . And anyway, I think the Terran ambassador was getting a little tired of having me around the embassy. He, uh, he seemed to be avoiding me as much as he could.'

Leoh barely suppressed a smile. 'Very well. Get your things together and you can move in with me today.'

'Good,' Hector said. And to himself he added, *I won't leave him for a minute. Then when Odal shows up I can protect him . . . and do what Geri wants me to.*

There was no escaping Hector. He moved into Leoh's apartment and stood within ten meters of the old scientist, day and night. When Leoh awoke, Hector was already whistling shrilly in the autokitchen, punching buttons, and somehow managing to make the automatic equipment burn at least one part of breakfast. Hector drove him wherever he wanted to go, and stayed with him when he got there. Leoh went to sleep with Hector's cheerful jabbering still in his ears.

Increasingly, they ate dinner at Geri Dulaq's sumptuous home on the outskirts of the city. Hector waggled like an overanxious puppy whenever Geri was in sight. And Leoh saw that she was coolly able to keep him at arm's length. There was something that she wanted Hector to do for her, the old man quickly realized, something Hector wouldn't talk about. Which – for Hector – was completely unusual.

About a week after the news of Odal's return, the Kerak major still hadn't been seen outside of his embassy's building. But an enterprising newsman, expecting new duels, asked for an interview with Leoh. The Professor met him at the dueling machine. Hector was at his side.

The newsman turned out to be Hector's age and Leoh's girth, florid in complexion, sloppy in dress, and slightly obnoxious in attitude.

'I know all about the basic principles of its operation,' he told Leoh airily when the Professor began to explain how the dueling machine worked.

'Oh? Have you had courses in psychonics?'

The newsman laughed. 'No, but I understand all about this dream-machine business.'

Pacing slowly by the empty control desk and peering up at the dueling machine's bulky consoles and power conditioners, he asked, 'How can you be sure that people can't be killed in this rig again? Major Odal actually killed people . . .'

'I understand the question,' Leoh said. 'I've added three new circuits to the machine. The first psychonically isolates the duelists inside the machine; it's now impossible for Odal or anyone else to contact the outside world while the machine is in operation.'

The newsman turned up the volume control on his wrist recorder. 'Go on.'

'The second circuit,' Leoh continued, 'monitors the entire duel. If either side requests, the dueling machine's chief medi-

112

tech can review the tape and determine if any rules were broken. Thus, even if there is foul play of some sort, we can at least catch it.'

'After the fact,' the newsman pointed out.

'Yes.'

'That wouldn't have helped Dulaq or Massan, or the others that were killed.'

Leoh could feel irritation growing inside him. 'After one duel, we could have found out what Odal was doing and stopped him.'

The newsman said nothing.

'Finally, we have added an automatic override to the medical monitoring equipment, so that if one of the duelists shows the slightest sign of actual medical danger, the duel is automatically stopped.'

The newsman thought it over for half a second. 'Suppose a man gets a sudden heart attack? He might be dead before you can get the door to his booth open, even though you've stopped the duel immediately.'

Leoh fumed. 'And if there's an earthquake, both duelists and much of the city may be destroyed. Young man, there is no way to make the world absolutely safe.'

'Maybe not.' But his round, puffed face showed he didn't believe it absolutely.

They talked for a quarter-hour more. Leoh showed him the equipment involved in the three new safety circuits and tried to explain how they worked. The newsman looked professionally skeptical and unimpressed. Leoh's exasperation mounted.

'Frankly, Professor, all you've told me is a lot of scientific mumbo jumbo. There's no guarantee that the machine won't kill people again.'

Reddening, Leoh snapped back, 'The *machine* didn't kill anyone! A man murdered his opponents, deliberately.'

'In the machine.'

'Yes, but it can't happen again!'

Shrugging, the newsman said, 'All I've got to go on is your word.'

'My reputation as a scientist means something, I should think.'

Hector interrupted. 'If the Acquatainian government is satisfied that the dueling machine's safe . . .'

The newsman laughed. 'Both the government and the Professor claimed the machine was absolutely safe when it was first installed here. Two men died in this gadget, and who knows how many others have been killed in Szarno and other places?'

'But that . . .'

Turning back to Leoh, he asked, 'How many people have been killed in dueling machines in the Commonwealth?'

'None !'

'You sure? I can check, you know.'

'Are you calling me a liar?'

'Look, it boils down to this: you told us the machine was safe, and two very important men were killed. Now you're saying it's safe again . . .' He let the implication dangle.

'Out !' Leoh snapped. 'Get out of here, or by all the ancient gods, old as I am . . .'

The newsman backed off a step. Then, 'Suppose I *am* doubting you. Not your veracity, but your optimism about the machine's being safe. Suppose I said you don't really know that it's safe, you're just hoping that it is.'

Hector stepped between them. 'Now wait . . . if you can't . . .'

'Suppose,' the newsman went on, ducking past Hector, 'suppose I challenged you to a duel.'

'I've used this machine many times,' Leoh said.

'Okay, but I still challenge you.'

Suddenly Leoh felt absolutely calm. 'Very well. I accept your challenge. And you can do whatever you want to during our duel to prove your point. But I insist on one condition: the tape of the duel must be made public knowledge immediately after the duel is finished.'

The newsman grinned. 'Perfect.'

Leoh realized that this was what he had been after all along.

*

Odal sat in his cell-like room in the Kerak embassy, waiting for the phone message. The room was narrow and severe, with strictly functional furniture – a bed, a desk and chair, a view screen. No decorations, plain military gray walls, no window.

Kor had explained the plan for Leoh's destruction before Odal had boarded the ship for Acquatainia. Odal did not like the plan, but it seemed workable and it would surely remove Leoh from the scene.

The phone buzzed.

Odal leaned across the desk and touched the ON button. The newsman's chubby face took form on the small screen.

'Well?' Odal demanded.

'He accepted the challenge. We duel in three days. And he wants the tape shown publicly, just as you thought he would.'

Odal smiled tightly. 'Excellent.'

'Look, if I'm going to be made to look foolish on that tape,' the newsman said, 'I think I ought to get more money.'

I don't handle the financial matters,' Odal said. 'You'll have to speak to the embassy accountant . . . *after* we see how well you play your part in the duel.'

Pouting, the newsman replied, 'All right. But I'm going to be finished for life when that tape is shown.'

'We'll take care of you,' Odal promised. *Indeed, we'll provide for you for the rest of your life.*

*

Geri Dulaq walked briskly out of the sunlight of the university's campus into the shadows of the dueling machine's high-vaulted chamber.

'Hector, you sounded so worried on the phone ...'

He took her hands in his. 'I am. That's why I wanted to talk to you. It's ... well, it's happened again. First Ponte argues the Professor into a duel, and now this newsman. You think Ponte might be working for Kerak, so ... I mean ...'

'Perhaps the newsman is too,' Geri finished for him.

Hector nodded. 'And with Odal back ... well, they're brewing up something ...'

'Where is the Professor now?' Geri asked.

Pointing to the office behind the dueling machine chamber, Hector said, 'In there. He doesn't want to be disturbed ... working on equations or something ... about interstellar ships, I think.'

Geri looked surprised.

'Oh, he's not worried about the duel,' Hector explained. 'I told him all about Ponte ... what you said, I mean. But he thinks the machine can't be tampered with, so he's not, uh, worried. And he beat Ponte pretty easily.'

Geri turned toward the massive, looming machine. 'I've never been here before. It's a little frightening.'

Hector put on a smile. 'There's nothing to be frightened about ... that is, I mean, well, it's only a machine. It can't hurt you.'

'I know. It was Odal and Kanus' hired monsters that killed father, not the machine itself.'

She walked along the long, curving, main control desk, looked over its banks of gauges and switches, ran a finger lightly across its plastisteel edge.

'Could you show me what it's like?'

Hector blinked. 'Huh?'

'In the dueling machine,' she said. 'Can it be used for something else, other than duels? I'd like to see what it's like to have your imagination made real.'

'Oh, but . . . well, you're not . . . I mean, nobody's supposed to run it without . . . that is . . .'

'You do know how to run the machine, don't you?' She looked right up into his eyes.

With a gulp, Hector managed a weak, 'Oh sure . . .'

'Then can't we use it together? Perhaps we can share a dream.'

Looking around, his hands suddenly clammy, Hector mumbled, 'Well, uh, somebody's supposed to be at the controls to, er, monitor the duel . . . I mean . . .'

'Just for a few little minutes?' Geri smiled her prettiest.

Hector melted. 'Okay . . . I guess it'll be all right. Just for a few minutes that is.'

He walked with her to the farther booth and helped her put on the neurocontacts. Then he went back to the main desk and with shaky hands set the machine into action. He checked and double-checked all the controls, pushed the final switches, and dashed to the other booth, tripping as he entered it and banging noisily into the seat. He sat down, fumbled with the neurocontacts hastily, and then stared into the screen.

Nothing happened.

For a moment he was panic-stricken. Then the screen began to glow softly, colors shifted, green mostly, soft cool green with a hint of blue in it . . .

And he found himself floating dreamily next to Geri in a world of green, with greenish light filtering down ever so softly from far above them.

'Hello,' Geri said.

He grinned at her. 'Hi.'

'I've always wondered what it would be like to be able to live underwater, without any equipment, like a mermaid.'

Hector noticed, when she said that, hundreds of fish swimming lazily about them. As his eyes adjusted to the subdued lighting, he saw sculptured shapes of coral about them, colors that he had never seen before.

'Our castle,' Geri said, and she swam slowly toward one of the coral pinnacles and disappeared behind it.

Hector found himself sliding easily after that. The water seemed to offer no resistance to his movement. He was completely relaxed, completely at home. He saw her up ahead, gliding gracefully along, and pulled up beside her. A great silver fish crossed in front of them, and brilliantly hued plants swayed gently in the currents.

'Isn't it beautiful?' Geri murmured. 'Our own world, without troubles, without dangers.'

Hector nodded. It was hard to believe that they were actually sitting in a pair of booths some thirty meters apart. Hard to admit that there was another world where a war was brewing, where Odal was waiting to commit another murder.

A dark shape slid out from behind the rocks ahead. Geri screamed.

It was Odal. Slim, dressed in black, his lean face a mask of death.

'Hector, don't let him! Hector, help me!'

Everything went black.

Hector snapped his eyes open. He was sitting in the booth beside Geri, his arms around her protectively. She was shuddering.

'How did . . .'

'It was my fault,' she gasped. 'I thought about Odal . . .'

The door to the booth was yanked open. Leoh stood there, his face a mixture of surprise and puzzlement.

'What are you two doing? All the lights and power in the building are off!'

'I'm sorry . . .' Hector began.

'It's my fault,' Geri said. She explained what happened.

Leoh still looked puzzled. 'But why are you both in the same booth?'

Hector started to answer then it hit him. 'I . . . I was in the other booth!'

'It's empty,' Leoh said. 'I looked in there first, when the power went off. The door was closed.'

Hector looked at Geri, then back at the Professor. 'I must've jumped out of the booth and ran over here . . . but, I mean . . . I don't remember doing it.'

The chief meditech came striding into the room, his steps clicking angrily against the hard flooring. 'What's going on here? Who blew out the power?'

Turning, Leoh said, 'It's all right, just a little experiment that didn't work out.'

The chief meditech looked over the control console in the fading sunlight of the afternoon as Geri and Hector got out of the booth. He muttered and glared at them.

'No permanent damage, I'm sure,' Leoh said as soothingly as he could.

The lights on the control panels sprang back to life, as did the room's main illumination lights. 'Hmp,' grunted the chief meditech. 'I guess it's all right. The power's on again.'

'I don't understand it,' Hector said.

'Neither do I,' Leoh answered. 'But it's something to think about.'

'What is?'

'How Hector got from one booth to the other.' To the chief meditech he called out, 'I'm going to take the tape of this, er, experiment. Do you mind?'

The chief meditech was still inspecting the machine with the aggresive solicitude of a worried father. He nodded curtly to Leoh, 'I don't think you should do any more such experiments until we have back-up power units installed. The entire building was blacked out.'

*

Leoh sat in his office behind the dueling machine room, staring at the now blank view screen. In three days he had run the tape at least a hundred times. He had timed it down to the picosecond. He had seen Geri and Hector swimming lazily, happily, like two humanized dolphins perfectly at ease in the

119

sea. Then Odal's shark-like form sliced into view. Geri screamed. The scene cut off.

It was precisely at that moment (within four picoseconds, as nearly as Leoh could calculate it) that the power in the whole building went off.

How long did it take Hector to get from his booth to Geri's? Thirty seconds? Leoh was looking into Hector's booth about thirty seconds after the power went off, he estimated. Less, then. Ten seconds? Physically impossible; no one could disconnect himself from the neurocontacts and spring from one booth to the other in ten seconds. And both booth doors were closed, too.

Leoh muttered to himself, 'Knowing Hector's manual dexterity, it's difficult to imagine him making the trip in less than ten minutes.'

All right then, he asked himself, *how did he get into Geri's booth? Precognition? He realized ahead of time that Odal would appear and frighten Geri? Then why doesn't he remember it, or even remember going from one booth to the other? And why the enormous power drain? What happened to the machine to cause it?*

There was only one answer that Leoh could see, but it was so farfetched that he wanted to find another one. The one answer was teleportation.

The dueling machine amplifies the powers of natural telepaths. Some telepaths have been reported to be able to move small objects with no apparent physical force. Could the dueling machine amplify that talent, too? And drain all the power in the building to do it?

Leoh shook his head. Too much theorizing, not enough facts. He wished there were tape cameras in the booths; then he could have timed Hector's arrival. Did he make the trip in four picoseconds? Or was it four-trillionths of a second?

The door slid open and Hector stood there uncertainly, his lanky form framed in the doorway.

Leoh looked up at him. 'Yes?'

'It's time . . . the, uh, newsman and his seconds are here for the duel.'

Feeling annoyed at the interruption, Leoh pushed himself out of the chair and headed for the dueling machine. 'A lot of silliness,' he muttered. 'Just a publicity stunt.'

The chief meditech, in his professional white cover-all now, introduced the duelists and their seconds. For Leoh, only Hector. For the newsman, his editor – a thin, balding, nervous type – and a network vice-president, who looked comfortable and well-fed. *Probably keeps three dietitians and a biochemist busy preventing him from going overweight*, Leoh groused to himself.

They exchanged formalities and entered the booths. Hector sat at one end of the long, curving padded bench that ran along the wall across the floor from the machine's control desk. The editor and V.P. sat at the other end. Except for the meditechs, who took their stations at the control consoles, there was no one else in the room. The press gallery was empty. The lights on the panels winked on. The silent room vibrated with the barely audible hum of electrical power.

In ten minutes, all the lights on the control panels flicked from green to amber. The duel was finished.

Hector shot up and started for Leoh's booth. The Professor came out, smiling slightly.

'Are you . . . did it go . . . all right?' Hector asked.

The newsman was getting out of the other booth. His editor put out a hand to steady him. The V.P. remained on the bench, looking half-disappointed, half-amused. The newsman seemed like a lumpy wad of dough, white-faced, shaken.

'He has terrible reflexes,' Leoh said, 'and no concept at all of the most elementary rules of physics.'

The V.P. got up from his seat and walked over toward Leoh, his hand extended and a toothy smile on his smooth face. 'Let me congratulate you, Professor,' he said in a hearty baritone.

Leoh took his hand, but replied, 'This has been nothing but

a waste of time. I'm surprised that a man in your position indulges in such foolishness.'

The V.P. bent his head slightly and answered softly, 'I'm afraid I'm to blame. My staff convinced me that it would be a good idea to test the dueling machine and then make the results of the test public. You have no objection if we run the tape of your duel on our tri-di broadcasts?'

With a shrug, Leoh said, 'Your man is going to look very foolish. He was run over by a bowling ball, and then over-estimated his strength and popped his back trying to lift ...'

The V.P. put up his hands. 'I don't care what the tape shows. I made up my mind to put it on the air, if you have no objections.'

'No, I don't object.'

'You'll become a famous man all over the planet,' the V.P. beamed. 'Your name will become a household word; tri-di stardom can do that for you.'

'If the tape will convince the Acquatainian people that the dueling machine is safe, fine,' Leoh said. 'As for fame ... I'm already rather well known.'

'Ah, but not to the general public. Certainly you're famous among your fellow scientists, and to the elite of Acquatainia and the Commonwealth. But all the general public's seen of you has been a few fleeting glimpses on news broadcasts. But now you're going to become *very* famous.'

'Because of one silly duel? I doubt that.'

'You'll see,' the V.P. promised.

*

The V.P. did not exaggerate. In fact, he had been overly conservative.

Leoh's duel was broadcast over the tri-di networks all across the planet that night. Within the week, it had been shown throughout the Acquataine Cluster and was in demand in the Commonwealth.

It was the first time a duel had ever been seen by the general public, and the fact that the inventor of the dueling machine was involved made it doubly fascinating. The sight of the chubby newsman bumbling into obvious traps and getting tangled in pulleys and inclined planes with bowling balls atop them, while Leoh solicitously urged him to be careful every step of the way, struck most people as funny. The Acquatainians, living for months now with the fear of war hanging over them, found a sudden and immense relief in Leoh's duel. Here was the inventor of the dueling machine, the man who had stopped the Kerak assassinations, appearing on tri-di, showing how clever he is, proving that Kerak is up against a mastermind.

The real facts of the matter – that Leoh had no influence with Martine's government, that Odal was now back in Acquatainia, that Kerak war fleets were quietly deploying along the Acquatainian frontier – these facts the average Acquatainian submerged in his joy over Leoh's duel.

Leoh became an instant public figure. He was invited to speak at every university in the Cluster. Tri-di shows vied for his appearance and newsmen followed his every move.

The old scientist tried to resist the pressure, at first. For the week after the original showing of his duel on tri-di, he refused to make any public statement.

'Tell them I'm busy,' he said to Hector, and he tried to barricade himself behind his equations and computer tapes in the office behind the dueling machine.

When the universities began calling on him, though, he bowed to their wishes. Before he knew it, he was swept away in a giddy tide of personal appearances, tri-di shows, and parties.

'Perhaps,' he told Hector, 'this is the way to meet the people who influence Martine's government. Perhaps I can convince them to consider the Commonwealth alliance, and they can put pressure on Martine.'

At parties, at private meetings, at press conferences, Leoh stressed the point. But there was no apparent effect. The students, the professors, the newsmen, the businessmen, the tri-di audience – they wanted entertainment, not politics. They wanted to be assured that all was well, not forced to think about how to protect themselves.

The university lectures were huge successes, as lectures. Leoh expected to be speaking mainly to the psychonics students, but each vast auditorium was filled to overflowing with students and faculty from political science, physics, mathematics, sociology, psychiatry ... thousands at each campus.

And at each university there were the local newsmen, tri-di appearances, discussion clubs. And the faculty parties in the evenings. And the informal student seminars in the late afternoons. And the newsman who just 'dropped in for a few words' at breakfast time.

It took more than two months to make the rounds of each university in the Cluster. At first, Leoh tried to steal a few moments each day to work on the problem of Hector's 'jump.' But each day he woke up more tired, each day was filled with still more people to talk to, people who listened respectfully, admiringly. Each night he retired later; happy, exhausted, with a small nagging grumble in the back of his mind that he should really stop this show-business routine and get back to science.

Hector grew more and more worried as he shepherded Leoh from one campus to the next. The old man was obviously enjoying himself hugely, and just as obviously spending too much of his strength on the traveling and personal appearances and parties. What's more, Geri was in the capital city, and all the eager smiling girls on all the campuses in the Cluster couldn't replace her in his eyes.

In the midst of all this, Leoh even fought two more duels.

The first one was with a university physics student who had bet his friends that he could beat the Professor. Leoh agreed good-naturedly to the duel, provided the boy was willing to let the tape be shown on tri-di. The boy agreed.

Instead of the simple physics arena, Leoh chose a more difficult battleground: the intensely warped space in the powerful gravitational field of a collapsed star. The duelists fought in a one-man spacecraft, using laser beams for weapons. The problem was to control the ship in a gravitational field so tenacious that one slip meant an inevitable spiral into the star's seething surface; and to aim the laser weapons properly, where the relativistic warp of space drove straightline physics out the window.

The boy tried bravely as the two ships circled the dying star. The tape showed the view from each ship, alternately. Now the viewer could see the black depths of space, empty except for a few distant pinpoints of stars, and the curving crescent of the other duelist's ship streaking by, a pencil beam of laser light flicking out, bending weirdly in that crazy gravity field, seeking its target. Then the bluish inferno of the star would slide into view, blazing, brilliant, drowning out everything else from sight.

The boy fought well, but finally maneuvered himself too close to the star. He could have escaped if he had controlled the ship a little better. Instead, he power-dived straight into its flaming surface. The tri-di executives decided to erase his final screams from the tape before they showed it to the public.

The second challenge came from an Acquatainian merchant, one of the richest men in the Cluster, who had drunk too much at a party and picked a quarrel with Leoh. The professor went back to the simple physics arena and disposed of him easily.

By the time Leoh (and Hector) returned to the capital, he was the darling of Acquatainian society. They feasted him, they toasted him, they took him to the ballet and opera, they did everything except let him alone to work. Geri was part of Acquatainia's social leadership, so Hector at least got to see her – but only in crowded, noisy rooms.

*

Odal sat tensely in his room's only chair and watched Kor's bullet-shaped head on the view screen as the Intelligence Minister said:

'So far the plan has gone extremely well. Leoh has not only been of no trouble to us, but his exploits have distracted most of the soft-headed Acquatainians. Meanwhile our preparations are exactly on schedule.'

'The invasion,' Odal murmured.

Kor smiled. 'We have – let us say, persuaded – the government of the Etra Domain to allow us to station a battle fleet in their territory. Etra stands between the Acquatainian Cluster and the nearest Star Watch bases. If the Commonwealth tries to intervene, we can hold up their forces long enough to allow us to conquer Acquatainia.'

Odal nodded curtly; he had heard the plan before.

'Now is the time,' Kor went on, 'for you to supply the final step. The destruction of Leoh, and the complete lulling of the Acquatainians.'

Odal said nothing.

'You still do not like the role you are required to play,' Kor said. 'No, don't bother to deny it, I can see it in your face. Let me remind you that your duty may not always be pleasant, but if you succeed your rewards will be high.'

'I will do my duty, unpleasant or not,' Odal said stiffly. *And I know the penalties for failure*, he added silently.

*

Leoh looked bone-weary to Hector as they returned from the party. That morning, a new psychonics building had been dedicated at the university. It was named the Albert Robertus Leoh Center for Psychonics Studies.

The day had been spent in speeches on an outdoor platform in the morning, a tour of the new building in the afternoon, dinner with the president and trustees of the university, and the inevitable party that night.

'I've simply got to find time,' Leoh was saying as they

stepped out of the lift tube into the hallway in front of their apartment, 'to run some experiments on your "jump". We can use the tape of . . .'

But Hector was staring quizzically at the apartment door. It was open and the lights inside were on.

'Another newsman, I'll bet,' Leoh said wearily.

'I'll tell him to come back some other time,' said Hector. He moved ahead of Leoh and entered the apartment.

Sitting on the air couch in the middle of the living-room was Odal.

'You!'

The Kerak major rose to his feet slowly, a tight smile on his face, as first Hector and then Leoh came in, saw him, and stopped.

'Good evening,' Odal said, getting to his feet. 'Come right in. After all, this is your place.'

'How did you get into? . . .'

'That's of no real concern. I'm here to settle some unfinished business. Professor Leoh, some time ago you accused me of cheating in the dueling machine. I was about to challenge you when the Watchman intervened. I challenge you now.'

'Now wait,' Hector began, 'you can't . . .'

'I already have. Professor, do you accept my challenge?'

Leoh stood three steps inside the door, unmoving, silent.

'Let me remind you,' Odal said calmly, 'that you have gone to great lengths to prove to the people of Acquatainia that the dueling machine is safe and harmless. If I may quote one of your many tri-di speeches, "Tampering with the dueling machine is a thing of the past". If you refuse to meet me in a duel, it will seem that you're afraid that the machine is not so safe . . . when I am the opponent.'

Leoh said, 'And you would, of course, see to it that my refusal became public knowledge.'

Smiling again, Odal nodded. 'You are a great celebrity. I'm sure the news media would learn about it one way or another.'

'Don't do it,' Hector said to Leoh. 'It's a trap. Don't agree to duel with him. I'll . . .'

'You, Watchman, have already beaten me in a duel,' Odal said, his smile vanishing. 'You can't ask me to face you again. It would be unfair.'

'I'll agree to the duel,' Leoh answered, 'if you'll agree to have the tape shown publicly.'

'Very well,' Odal said. 'We will meet in three days, as is customary?'

'Make it a week,' Hector said. 'Give us a chance to . . . uh, inspect the machine and make sure, that is . . .'

'Make certain that the monsters from Kerak haven't tampered with it?' Odal laughed. 'Very well, a week from today.'

Odal walked toward the door, stepped between Hector and Leoh, and left. The door clicked shut behind him.

Hector turned his eyes from the closed door to Leoh. 'You shouldn't have accepted . . . I mean, well, it's a trick of some kind, I know it is.'

The Professor looked thoughtful. 'Is it? Or is Odal – or Kanus, or whoever – getting desperate? I've been able to show the Acquatainian people that they have nothing to fear from the dueling machine, you know. They might be trying to restore the machine to its symbol of terror.'

Hector shook his head.

'But I can beat Odal in a fair duel,' Leoh said. 'After all, I've won every duel I've fought, haven't I? And you beat Odal. The only duels he won were when he had outside help. I think I can beat him, I honestly do.'

Hector didn't answer, but merely stared in disbelief at the old man.

*

The building that housed the dueling machine was surrounded with throngs of people. Their restless, anxious murmuring could be heard even inside the normally quiet room. The press gallery, high above the machine itself, was packed with reporters.

For a solid week every tri-di outlet in the Acquataine Cluster had drummed continuously on the coming duel between Leoh and Odal. Good against evil, with the issue seriously in doubt. The old, overweight, shaggy professor against the blade-slim professional killer.

Hector and Leoh stood before the machine. The meditechs were bustling about making final checks on the controls. On the other side of the room, tiers of temporary seats had been put in. They were filled with government and social leaders, military men, policemen, and a small contingent from the Kerak embassy. Geri Dulaq sat in the front row, next to the empty chair that would be Hector's.

'I still don't like it,' Hector said in a near whisper to Leoh.

With his eyes sweeping the room, watching the restless onlookers and the busy meditechs, Leoh answered, 'Relax, my boy. We've turned the machine inside out. The worst he can do is to defeat me. At the slightest medical irregularity, the machine will automatically stop us. And besides, I still think I can beat him. I'll be using the neutron star environment again, the same one I used against that college student. He'll have no advantage over me there.'

A roar went up from the crowd outside.

'Here he comes,' Hector said.

The main doors opened. Flanked by two rows of uniformed policemen, in walked Odal and his two seconds, all in the light blue uniforms of Kerak. Odal was annoyedly brushing something from his tunic.

'Evidently,' Leoh said, 'diplomatic immunity didn't protect Odal entirely from the crowd.'

The introductions, the medical checks, the instructions, the choice of weapons and environment – all seemed to take hours instead of minutes. Until suddenly they were over, and Hector found himself walking alone to his spectator's seat.

He sat beside Geri and watched Leoh and Odal enter their booths, watched the meditechs take their stations at the control desks watched the panel lights turn from amber to green. The duel was on.

The crowd stirred uncertainly. A buzzing murmur filled the room. There was nothing to do now but wait.

Geri leaned close to Hector and asked sweetly, 'Did you bring a gun?'

'Huh? A . . . what for? I mean . . .'

She whispered, 'For Odal. I have a small one in my handbag.'

'But . . . but . . .'

'You promised me!' Still in a whisper, but harsher now.

'I know, but not here. There're . . . well, there're too many people here. Someone might get hurt . . . if shooting starts . . .'

Geri thought a moment. 'Maybe you're right. Of course, if he kills Professor Leoh in there, he'll walk right out of here and board a Kerak star ship and we'll never see him again.'

Hector couldn't think of a reply, so he just sat there feeling thoroughly miserable.

The two of them remained silent for the rest of the half-hour. At the end of the time limit for the duel, all the lights on the machine went amber. The crowd let out a gust of disappointed-yet-relieved sighs. Hector sprinted to Leoh's booth while Odal's seconds marched in time to his.

Leoh came out of the booth looking very thoughtful.

'You're all right?' Hector asked.

'What? Oh yes, fine. He played exactly by the rules,' Leoh said. He looked toward Odal, who was smiling icily, calm and confident. 'He played extremely well . . . extremely well. There were a couple of times when I thought he'd really finish me off. And I never really put him into much trouble at all.'

The chief meditech was motioning for the two duelists to come to him at the main control desk. Hector accompanied Leoh.

'The first part of the duel has been a draw,' the chief meditech said. 'You – both of you – now have the option of with-drawing for a day, or continuing the duel now.'

'I will continue,' Odal said unhesitatingly.

Leoh nodded, 'Continue.'

'Very well,' said the chief meditech. Turning to Odal, 'Yours is the choice of environment and weapon. Are there any special instructions necessary?'

Odal shook his head. 'The Professor knows how to drive a ground car?' At Leoh's affirming nod he said, 'Then that is all the skill that is necessary.'

*

Leoh found himself sitting at the wheel of a sleek blue ground car: plastic-bubble canopy, two bucket seats, engine throb-bing under an aerodynamically sculptured hood.

Ahead of him stretched a highway, arrow-straight to the horizon, where jagged bluish mountains rose against the harsh yellow sky. The car pulled off to the side of the road, in neutral gear. The landscape around the highway was bleak – desert – flat, featureless, cloudless and hot.

Odal's voice came from the radio in the dashboard. 'I am parked about five kilometres behind you, Professor. You will pull out onto the highway and I will follow you. These cars have wheels, not air cushions; there are no magnetic bumpers, no electronic controls to lock you onto the highway. A few kilometers ahead, as we enter the mountains, the road becomes quite interesting. The object of the game, of course, is to make the other fellow crash. But if you can outrun me for a half hour, I will acknowledge you as the winner.'

Leoh glanced at the controls, touched the drive button, and nudged the throttle. The turbine purred smoothly. He swung onto the highway and ran up to a hundred kilometers per hour. The rearview screen showed a blood-red car, exactly like his own except for its color, pulling up precisely ten car lengths behind him.

'I'll let you get the feel of the car while we're on the

straightaway,' Odal's voice came through the radio. 'We won't begin to play in earnest until we get into the mountains.'

The road was rising now, Leoh realized. A gentle grade, but at their speed they were soon well above the desert floor. The mountains were no longer distant blue wrinkles; they loomed close, high, and bareboned, with scraggy bushes and sparse patches of grass on them.

Leoh nearly missed the first curve, it came on him so quickly. He cut to the inside, slammed on the brakes, and skidded around.

'Not very good,' Odal laughed.

The red car was just off his left rear fender now, crowding him against the shoulder of the mountain rise that jutted up from the right side of the road. Leoh could hear pebbles clattering against the floorboards, over the whine of their two turbines. On the other side of the road, the cliff dropped away to the desert floor. And they were still climbing.

Leoh hugged the right side of the road, with Odal practically beside him. Suddenly the mountains fell away and a bridge, threaded dizzily between two cliffs, stood before them. It seemed to Leoh that the bridge was leaping toward him. He tried to get back toward the center of the road, but Odal rammed his side. The wheel ripped out of his hands, spinning wildly. The car skidded toward the road's shoulder. Leoh grabbed at the wheel, steered out of the skid, and found himself on the bridge, the supporting suspension cables whizzing past. He was sweating hard and hunched, white-knuckled, over the wheel.

Odal was in front of him now. *He must've passed me when I skidded*, Leoh told himself. The red car was running smoothly, easily; Odal waved one hand back to his opponent.

On the other side of the bridge the road became a torturous series of curves, climbs, and drops. The grades were steep, the turns murderous, and at times the road narrowed so much that two cars could barely squeeze by. Sometimes they were flanked on both sides by looming masses of rock, rising up out of sight. Mostly, though, one side of the road was a sheer drop of a thousand meters or more.

Odal braked, swerved, pulled up alongside Leoh and slammed the two cars together with bone-rattling force. He was trying to force Leoh off the edge of the cliff. Leoh clung to the wheel, fighting for control. His one defense was that he could set the speed for the battle; but to his horror he found that not even this was under his real control. The car refused to slow much past seventy-five.

'You wish to stop and enjoy the scenery?' Odal called to him, banging the two cars together again, pushing Leoh dangerously close to the cliff's edge.

Desperately, Leoh leaned on the throttle with all his weight. The car spurted ahead, leaving Odal momentarily in a cloud of wheel-churned dirt.

'Ah-hah, now the turtle becomes a rabbit!' The red car streaked after him.

There was a tunnel ahead. Leoh raced for it, praying that it was long enough and narrow enough for him to stay ahead of Odal. *The time must be running out. It's got to be!* It was hard for Leoh to keep his sweaty hands firm on the wheel. His back and head were hurting, his heart racing dangerously.

The tunnel was long and straight – and narrow! Hopefully, Leoh planted his car in the middle of the roadway and throttled down as much as he could. Still, the tunnel walls were a blur as he roared by, the turbine echoing shrilly against the encasing rock.

The red car was pulling close and now it was trying to pass him. Leoh swerved slightly to the left, to block it. The red car moved right. Leoh edged that way. Odal cut left again.

Got to keep ahead of him. Time must be almost over. Odal was insisting on his left. Leoh pushed farther to the left, staying ahead of him. But Odal kept coming, up off the roadway and onto the curving tunnel wall with his left wheels.

Leoh stayed on the left of the road and Odal swung even farther up the wall just behind Leoh's fender.

Glancing at the rearview screen, Leoh could see Odal's face clenched grimly, determined to pass him. The red car seemed to climb halfway up the curving tunnel wall and . . .

And then fell over, out of control, smashing over upside down onto the roadway, exploding in a shower of sparks and fuel with a concussion that slammed Leoh so hard he nearly lost control of his car.

He found himself sitting in the dueling machine booth, the screen before him a calm flat gray, his body soaking wet, his hands pressed into aching fists in front of him, as though he were still gripping the car's steering wheel.

The door jerked open and Hector ducked into the booth, his face anxious.

'You're all right?'

Leoh's arms dropped and his whole body relaxed.

'I beat him,' he said. 'I beat Odal!'

They stepped outside the booth, Leoh smiling broadly now. Across the way, Odal's thin face was deathly grim. The crowd was absolutely still, not daring to believe what it saw.

The chief meditech cleared his throat and announced loudly, 'Professor Leoh is the victor!'

The crowd's sudden roar burst through the room. They rose from their seats, swarmed down upon the machine and lifted Leoh and Hector to their shoulders. Jumping up and down on the main control desk, yelling louder than anyone, was the white-coated chief meditech. Outside, the much larger throng was cheering even harder.

Within a few minutes no one was left in the chamber except a few of the uniformed policemen, Odal, and his seconds.

'Are you able to go outside now?' asked one of the soldiers, also a major.

The taut expression on Odal's face relaxed a little. 'Of course.'

The three men walked from the building to a waiting

ground car. The other soldier, a colonel, said to Odal, 'You have taken your death rather well.'

'Thank you.' Odal managed a thin smile. 'But after all, it's not as though I was killed by the enemy. I engaged in a suicide mission, and my mission has been accomplished.'

*

'I ... well ... you saw what happened,' Hector said to Geri. 'How could anybody do anything in that mob?'

They were sitting together in a restaurant near the tri-di studio where Leoh was being lionized by a panel of Acquatainia's leading citizens.

She poked at her food with a fork and said, 'You might never get the chance to kill him again. He's probably on his way back to Kerak right now.'

'Well, maybe that's ... I mean ... murder just isn't right ...'

'It wouldn't be murder,' Geri said coldly, staring at her plate. 'It would be an execution. Odal deserves to die! And if you won't do it, I'll find someone who can!'

'Geri ... I ...'

'If you really loved me, you'd have done it already.' She looked as though she was going to cry.

'But it's ...'

'You promised me!'

Hector sagged, defeated. 'All right, don't cry. I'll ... I'll think of something.'

*

Odal sat now in the office of the Kerak ambassador. The ambassador had left discreetly when Kor's call came through.

The Kerak major sat at a huge desk, leaning back comfortably in the soft padding of the luxurious leather swivel chair. The wall-sized view screen across the room seemed to dissolve into another room: Kor's dimly lit office. The Intelligence Minister eyed Odal for a long moment before speaking.

'You seem relieved.'

'I have performed an unpleasant duty, and done it successfully,' Odal said.

'Yes, I know. Leoh is now serving us to his full capacity. The Acquatainians will look up to him now as their savior. The fear they felt of Major Par Odal is now dissolved, and with it, their fear of Kerak is also purged. They associate Leoh with safety and victory. And while they are toasting him and listening to his pompous speeches, we will strike!'

Even though his presence in the room was only an image, Odal saw clearly what was in Kor's mind: bigger prisons, more prisoners, more interrogation rooms filled with terrified, helpless people who would cringe at the mention of Kor's name.

'Now then,' Kor said, 'new duties await you, Major. Not quite so unpleasant as committing suicide. And these duties will be performed here in Kerak.'

Odal said evenly, 'I would not wish to interrogate other army officers again.'

'I realize that,' Kor replied, frowning. 'That phase of our investigation is finshed. But there are other groups that must be examined. You would have no objection, I trust, to interrogating diplomats ... members of the Foreign Ministry?'

Romis' people? Odal thought. *Kor must be insane. Romis won't stand for having his people arrested.*

'Yes, Romis,' Kor answered the major's unspoken question. 'Who else would have the pigheaded pride to lead the plotting against the Leader?'

Or the intelligence, Odal found himself thinking. Aloud he asked, 'When do I return to Kerak?'

'Tomorrow morning a ship will be ready for you.'

Odal nodded. *Then I have only tonight to find the Watchman and crush him.*

*

Hector paced nervously along the narrow control booth of the tri-di studio. Technicians and managers bent over the monitors and electronic gear. Behind them, shadowed in the dimly lit booth, were a host of visitors whom Hector elbowed and jostled as he fidgeted up and down.

Beyond the booth's window wall was the well-lit studio where Leoh sat flanked by a full dozen of Acquatainia's leading newsmen and political philosophers.

The old man looked very tired but very pleased. The show had started by running the tape of the duel against Odal. Then the panel members began questioning Leoh about the duel, the machine itself, his career in science, his whole life.

Hector turned from the studio to peer into the crowd of on-lookers in the dimly lit control booth. Geri was still there, off by the far corner, squeezed between an old politician and a slickly dressed female advertising executive. Geri was still pouting. Hector turned away before she saw him watching her.

'It seems clear,' one of the political pundits was saying out in the studio, 'that Kanus can't use the dueling machine to frighten us any more. And without fear, Kanus isn't half the threat we thought he was.'

'I disagree,' Leoh said, shifting his bulk in the frail-looking web chair. 'Kerak has made great strides in isolating Acquatainia diplomatically . . .'

'But we never depended on our neighbors for our own defense,' a newsman said. 'Those so-called allies of ours were more of a drain on our treasury than a help to us.'

'But Kerak now has the industrial base of Szarno and outposts that flank Prime Minister Martine's new defense line.'

'Kerak would never dare attack us, and if they did, we'd beat them just as we did the last time.'

'But an alliance with the Commonwealth . . .'

'We don't need it. Kanus is a paper tiger, believe me. All bluff, all dueling machine trickery, but no real strength. He'll probably be deposed by his own people in another year or two.'

Something made Hector shift his gaze from the semi-circle of sonorous solons to the technical crews working the cameras and laser lights. Something made him squint into the pooled shadows far in the back of the studio, where a single tall, slim man stood. Hector couldn't see his face, or what he was wearing, or the colour of his hair. Only the knife-like outline of a figure that radiated danger: Odal.

Without thinking twice about it, Hector pushed past the crowd in the control booth toward the door. He stepped on toes and elbowed technicians in the backs of their heads in his haste to get out into the studio, leaving a wake of muttering, sore-rubbing people behind him. He went right past Geri, who stepped back out of his way but refused to say anything to him or even look directly into his eyes.

The door from the control booth led into a small entryway that had two more doors in it: one to the outside hallway and one to the studio. A uniformed guard stood before the studio door.

'I'm sorry, sir, you can't go in while the show's in progress.'

'But . . . I saw someone come in the back way . . . into the studio . . .'

Shrugging, the guard said, 'Must be a member of the camera crew. No one else allowed in.'

Hector blinked once, then went to the hall door. The corridor outside circled the studio. At least, he thought it did. He followed it around. Sure enough, there was another door with a blinking red light atop it, labeled STUDIO C. Hector pushed the door open. Inside, in the focus of a circle of lights and cameras, a man and woman were locked in a wild embrace.

'Hey, who opened the door?'

'Cut! CUT! Get that clown out of here! Can't even tape a simple scene without tourists wandering into the studio! Of all the . . .'

Hector quickly shut the door, closing off a string of invective that would have made his old drillmaster back at the Star Watch Academy grin with appreciation.

Which studio are they in?

138

As if in answer, farther down the hall a door opened and Odal stepped out. He was not in uniform; instead he wore a simple dark tunic and slacks. But it was unmistakably Odal. He glanced directly at Hector, a sardonic smile on his lips, then started walking the other way. Hector chased after him, but Odal disappeared around a bend in the almost featureless corridor.

A door was closing farther down the hall. Hector sprinted to it and yanked it open. The room was dark. He stepped in.

In the faint light from the hallway, Hector saw row after row of life-sized tri-di viewscreens, each flanked by a desk of control and monitoring equipment. *A tape viewing room,* he reasoned. *Or maybe an editing room.*

He walked hesitantly toward the center of the room. It was big, filled with the bulky screens and desks. Plenty of room to hide in. The door snapped shut behind him, plunging the room into total darkness.

Hector froze rock-still. Odal was in here. He could feel it. Gradually his eyes grew accustomed to the darkness. He turned slowly and began retracing his steps toward the door, only to bump into a chair and send it clattering into its desk.

'You defeated me in the dueling machine,' Odal's voice echoed calmly through the room. 'Now let's see if you can defeat me in real life. This room is soundproof. We are alone. No one will disturb us.'

'Uh ... I'm unarmed,' Hector said. It was hard to trace the source of Odal's voice. The echoes spoiled any chance of locating him in the darkness.

'I'm also unarmed. But we are both trained fighting men. You have no doubt had standard Star Watch hand-to-hand combat training.'

The painful memory of fumbling through the rough-and-tumble courses at the Star Watch Academy surged through Hector's mind. What he remembered most vividly was laying flat on his back with his instructor screaming. 'No, no, *no!*' at him.

Odal stepped out from behind a full-length view screen. 'You seem less than eager to do battle with me. Let me demonstrate my qualifications.'

Odal's foot lashed into one of the desk chairs, smashing its fragile frame against the tough plastic of the view screen. The chair disintegrated. Then he swung an edge-of-the-hand chop at the top of the nearby desk: the metal dented with a loud *crunk*!

Hector backed away until he felt another desk pressing against his legs. He glanced behind him and saw that it was some sort of master control unit, long and filled with complicated switches and monitor screens. Several roller chairs lined its length.

Odal was advancing on him. Something in the back of Hector's mind was telling him to run away and hide, but then he heard the barking voice of his old instructor insisting, 'The best defense is a fast, aggressive attack.' Hector took a deep breath, planted his feet solidly, and launched himself at Odal.

Only to find himself twisted around, lifted off his feet, and thrown back against the desk, banging painfully against the switches.

'LOOKING FOR THE IDEAL VACATION PARADISE?' a voice boomed at them. From behind Odal's shoulder a girl in a see-through spacesuit did a free-fall somersault. Hector blinked at her, and Odal looked over his shoulder, momentarily amazed. The voice blared on, 'JOIN THE FUN CROWD AT ORBIT HOUSE, ACQUATAINIA'S NEWEST ZERO-GRAVITY-RESORT...'

Through his mind flashed another maxim from his old instructor: 'Whenever possible, divert your opponent's attention. Create confusion. Feint, maneuver!'

Hector rolled off the desk top and ran along the master control unit, pounding every switch in sight.

'TIRED OF BEING CALLED SHORTY?' A disgruntled young man, standing on tiptoes next to a gorgeous, statuesque redhead, appeared beside Odal. The Kerak major involuntarily stepped back.

'THE IRRESISTIBLE PERFUME,' a seductive blonde materialized before his eyes, speaking smokily.

'MODERN SCIENCE CAN CURE ANY DISEASE, BUT WHEN EMBARRASSING ...' said a medic, radiating sincerity and concern.

Odal was surrounded by solid-looking, life-sized, tri-di advertising pitches.

'WHEN YOU'VE EATEN MORE THAN YOU SHOULD ...'
'THE NORMAL TENSIONS OF MODERN LIFE ...'
'FOR THE ULTIMATE IN FEMININE ...'

Eyes goggling, Odal saw himself being pressed backward by a teenage dancer, an 'average family' mother, a worried young husband, a nervous businessman, a smiling teen couple, a crowd of surfers, a chorus of animated vegetables. Suddenly bellowing with rage, Odal dived through the pleading, cajoling, urgent figures and threw himself at the long control desk.

'You can't hide from me!' he roared, and he started punching at the control switches, banging the desk panels with both fists.

'Who's hiding?' Hector yelled from behind him.

Odal turned and swung heavily at the voice. Startled, he saw his fist whisk through the impalpable jaw of a lovely girl in a skimpy bathing suit. She smiled at him and continued selling. '... AND WHEN YOU'RE IN THE MOOD FOR SOMETHING REALLY REFRESHING ...'

Hector had ducked away. Odal turned and chased after the Watchman, trying to follow him as he flickered in and out among the dozens of tri-di images that were dancing, urging, laughing, drinking, eating, taking pills, worrying ...

'You coward!' Odal screamed over the babble of sales talk.

'Why should I fight you?' Hector hollered back from somewhere across the room.

Odal squinted, trying to see through the gyrating tri-di figures. 'You tricked me in the dueling machine but now there'll be no tricks. I'll find you, and when I do, I'll kill you !'

The flash of a black-and-silver uniform among the fashion models, overweight women, underweight men, scientific demonstrations and new, new, new products. Odal headed in that direction.

'And what about Leoh?' Hector's voice cut through the taped noise. 'He killed you without any tricks. But you're afraid to go after him now, aren't you?'

Odal laughed. 'Do you really believe that old man beat me? I could have destroyed him at any time I wished.'

He ducked under the arm of a well-preserved matron who was saying, 'WHY LET ADVANCING AGE WORRY YOU, WHEN A REJUVE ...' There was Hector, edging slowly toward the door.

'You deliberately lost to Leoh?' Hector's face, in the reflections of the tri-di images, looked more puzzled than frightened. 'To make it seem ...'

'To make it seem that Leoh is a great hero, and that Kerak is populated by weaklings and cowards. All his duels were designed for that purpose. And while he lulls the Acquatainians with his tales of victory, we prepare to *strike*.'

On the final word Odal leaped at Hector, hit him with satisfying solidity, shoulder in mid-section, and they both went down.

A tangle of arms and legs, knees and elbows, gasps, two strong young bodies grappling. Somehow they rolled into one of the desk chairs, which toppled down on them. Odal felt Hector slipping out of his grasp. As the Kerak major started to get back to his feet, the chair slid into him again and he slipped against it and hit the floor face first.

Swearing, he started to get up. But Hector was already on his feet. And then the door swung open, stabbing light from the hallway into the room. A girl stood there, with a gun in her trembling hand.

'Hector ! Here !' Geri said, and she tossed the gun to the Watchman.

Hector grabbed it and pointed it at Odal. The Kerak major froze, on one knee, hands on the floor, head upturned, face a mask of rage turned to sudden fear. Hector stood equally immobile, arm outstretched with the gun aimed at Odal's head.

'Kill him!' Geri whispered harshly. 'Quickly, they're coming!'

Hector let his arm relax. The gun dropped slightly away from Odal. 'Get up,' he said. 'And ... don't give me any excuses for using this thing.'

Odal got slowly to his feet.

'Kill him! You promised!' Geri insisted, half in tears.

'I can't ... not like this ...'

'You mean you won't!'

Nodding without taking his eyes off Odal, Hector said, 'That's right, I won't. Not even for you.'

Odal's voice was like a knife. 'You'd better kill me, Watchman, while you have the chance. I'll spend the rest of my life hunting you.'

A trio of uniformed guards puffed up to the doorway; behind them were a half-dozen people from the tri-di show, and Leoh.

'What's going on? Who's this? Are you ...'

'This is Major Odal,' Hector said, pointing with the gun. 'He's ... uh, under the protection of diplomatic immunity. Please escort him back to the Kerak embassy.'

His face expressionless, Odal nodded to the Star Watchman and went with the guards.

*

'You mean it all went out on the tri-di network? Every word?' asked Hector.

He, Leoh, and Geri were sitting in the back of an automated Dulaq ground car as it threaded its way through the darkened city, heading for Geri's home. The midnight rain was falling for its programed half-hour, so the car's bubble top was up.

Geri had not said a word since Odal was taken from the tri-di studio.

But Leoh was chuckling. 'When you hit all those switches and turned on the commercial tapes, you also turned on the sound system for every studio. We heard the bedlam, with you and Odal shouting at each other over it all. It came over the speakers right in the middle of our show. You should have seen the look on everyone's face! And I understand that you ruined at least six other shows that were being taped at the time.'

'Really?' Hector squirmed. 'I . . . that is, I didn't mean . . . well, I'm sorry about that . . .'

Waving a hand at him, Leoh said, 'Relax, my boy. Your fight with Odal – the audio portion of it – was beamed into nearly every home on the planet. Everyone in Acquatainia knows what a fool I've been, and that Kerak is still as much of a threat as ever.'

'You're not a fool,' Hector said.

'Yes, I've been one,' insisted Leoh. 'Worse, I've been a dupe, letting my own glory get in the way of my judgment. But that's over now. My place is in science not politics, and certainly not show business! I'm going to concentrate on your "jump" in the dueling machine. If that was a sample of teleportation, then the machine can amplify that talent, just as it amplified Odal's telepathic abilities. Now, if we put enough power in to the machine . . .'

The car glided to a stop under the roofed driveway in front of the entrance to Geri's house. Leoh stayed in the car while Hector walked her to her door. In the shadows, he couldn't see her face too well. They stopped at the door.

'Um . . . Geri, I . . . well, I just couldn't kill him. Not . . . not like that. I wanted to please you . . . but, well, if you want an assassin . . . I guess it's just not me that you're interested in.'

She said nothing. A gentle warm breeze brought the odor of wet leaves to them.

Hector fidgeted.

Finally he said, 'Well, good night . . .'

'Good-by, Hector,' Geri said flatly.

Leoh was studiously looking the other way, watching the final few drops of rain splatter on the statuary alongside the driveway, when Hector returned to the car. The old scientist looked at the Watchman as he ducked into the car and slumped in the seat.

'Why so glum, my boy? What's the matter?'

Shrugging, Hector said, 'It's a long story . . .'

'Oh, I see. Well then. To get back to the teleportation idea. If we can boost the power of the machine . . .'

The Farthest Dream

It was ironic, thought Odal, that they were using the dueling machine to torture him. For it was torture, no matter what they called it or how they smiled when they were doing it.

He sat there in the cramped cubicle, staring at its featureless walls, the blank view screen, waiting for them to begin.

The price of failure was heavy, too heavy. Kanus had made Odal the glory of Kerak while he was a success, while he was killing the enemies of Kerak.

Now they were killing him.

Not that they caused him any physical harm. He was not even under arrest, technically. Merely assigned to experimentation at Kor's headquarters, the Ministry of Intelligence: a huge, stone, hilltop castle, ancient and brooding from the outside; inside, a maze of pain and terror and Kor's swelling lust for victims.

In the dueling machine, the illusion of pain was no less agonizing that the real thing. Odal smiled sardonically. The men he had killed died first in their imaginations. But soon enough their hearts stopped beating.

Now then, are you ready? It was a voice in his mind, put there by the machine's circuitry through the neurocontacts circling his head.

We are going to probe a bit deeper today, in an effort to find the source of your extrasensory talents. I advise you to relax and cooperate.

There had been three of them working on him yesterday, from the other side of the machine. Today, Odal could tell, there were more. Six? Eight? A dozen possibly.

He felt them: foreign thoughts, alien personalities, in his own mind. His hands twitched uncontrollably and his body began to ache and heave.

They were seizing his control centers, battering at sensory complexes. Muscles cramped spasmodically, nerves screamed in anguish, body temperature soared, ears shrilled, eyes flashed flaming reds and unbearable star bursts. Now they were going deeper, beyond the physical effects, digging, clawing away through a life-time of self-protective neural patterns, reaching down with a searing, white-hot, twelfth-power probe into the personality itself.

Odal heard a terrified voice howling, *They're after ME. They're trying to get ME. Hide! Hide!*

The voice was his own.

*

Despite its spaciousness, Leoh thought, the Prime Minister's office was a stuffy antique of a room, decorated in blue and gold, with the weight of outmoded traditions and useless memories hanging more heavily than the gilt draperies that bordered each door and window.

The meeting had been small and unspectacular. Martine had invited Leoh for an informal chat, Hector was pointedly not invited. A dozen or so aides, politicians, and administrators clustered around the Prime Minister's desk as he officially thanked Leoh for uncovering Kerak's attempt to use the dueling machine as a smoke screen for their war preparations.

'It was Star Watch Lieutenant Hector who actually uncovered the plot, not me,' Leoh insisted.

Martine waved away the words impatiently. 'The Watchman is merely your aide; you are the man that Kanus fears.'

After about ten minutes of talking, Martine nodded to one of his aides, who went to a door and admitted a covey of news photographers. The Prime Minister stood up and walked around his desk to stand beside Leoh, towering proudly over the old man, while the newsmen took their pictures.

Then the meeting broke up. The newsmen left and everyone else began to drift out of the office.

'Professor Leoh.'

He was nearly at the doorway when Martine called. Leoh turned back and saw the Prime Minister sitting at his tall desk chair. But instead of his usual icy aloofness, there was a warm, almost friendly smile on Martine's face.

'Please close the door and sit down with me for a few minutes more,' Martine said.

Puzzled, Leoh did as the Prime Minister asked. As he took an armchair off to one side of the desk, he watched Martine carefully run a hand over the communications panel set into his desk top. Then the Prime Minister opened a drawer in the desk and Leoh heard the tiny click of a switch being turned.

'There. Now I'm sure that we're alone. That switch isolates the room completely. Not even my private secretary can listen to us now.'

Leoh felt his eyebrows rising toward his scalp.

'You have every right to look surprised, Professor. And I should look apologetic and humble. That's why I had to make certain that this meeting is strictly private.'

'*This* meeting?' Leoh echoed. 'Then the meeting we just had, with the others and the newsmen . . .'

Martine smiled broadly. 'Kanus is not the only one who can put up a smoke screen.'

'I see. Well, what did you want to tell me?'

'First, please convey my apologies to Lieutenant Hector. He was not invited here for reasons that will be obvious in a moment. I realize that he wormed the truth out of Odal, although I'm not convinced that he knew what he was doing when he did it.'

Leoh suppressed a chuckle. 'Hector has his own way of doing things.'

Nodding, Martine went on more soberly. 'Now then, the real reason for my wanting to speak to you privately : I have been something of a stubborn fool. I realize that now. Kanus has not only outwitted me, but has actually penetrated deeply into my government. When I realized that Lal Ponte is a Kerak agent ...' The Prime Minister's face was grim.

'What are you going to do with him?'

A shrug. 'There's nothing I can do. He has been implicated indirectly by Odal. There's no evidence, despite a thorough investigation. But I'm sure that if Kanus conquered the Acquataine Cluster, Ponte would expect to be named Prime Minister of the puppet government.'

Leoh said nothing.

'Ponte is not that much of a problem. He can be isolated. Anything that I want from his office I can get from men I know I can trust. Ponte can sit alone at his desk until the ceiling caves in on him.'

'But he's not your only problem.'

'No. It's the military problem that threatens us most directly. You and Spencer have been right all along. Kerak is building swiftly for an attack and our defensive build-up is too far behind them to be of much use.'

'Then the alliance with the Commonwealth ...'

Shaking his head unhappily, Martine explained, 'No, that's still impossible. The political situation here is too unstable. I was voted into office by the barest margin ... thanks to Ponte. To think that I was elected because Kanus wanted me to be! We've both been pawns, Professor.'

'I know.'

'But, you see, if Dulaq and Massan and all their predecessors never allied Acquatainia with the Commonwealth, then for me to attempt it would be an admission of weakness. There are strong pro-Kerak forces in the legislature, and many others who are still as blind and stubborn as I've been. I would be voted out of office in a week if I tried to make an alliance with the Terrans.'

Leoh asked, 'Then what can you do?'

'I can do very little. But you can do much. I cannot call the Star Watch for help. But you can contact your friend, Sir

149

Harold, and suggest that he ask me for permission to bring a Star Watch fleet through the Cluster. Any excuse will do . . . battle maneuvers, exploration, cultural exchange, anything.'

Leoh shifted uneasily in his chair. 'You want me to ask Harold to ask you . . .'

'Yes, that's it.' Martine nodded briskly. 'And it must be a small Star Watch fleet, quite small. To the rest of Acquatainia, it must appear obvious that the Terran ships are not being sent here to help defend us against Kerak. But to Kanus, it must be equally obvious that he cannot attack Acquatainia without the risk of killing Watchmen and immediately involving the Commonwealth.

'I think I understand,' said Leoh, with a rueful smile. 'Einstein was right: nuclear physics is much simpler than politics.'

Martine laughed, but there was bitterness in it.

*

Kanus sat in brooding silence behind his immense desk, his thin, sallow face dark with displeasure. Sitting with him in the oversized office, either looking up at him at his cunningly elevated desk, or avoiding his sullen stare, were most of the members of his Inner Cabinet.

At length, the Leader spoke. 'We had the Acquataine Cluster in our grasp, and we allowed an old refugee from a university and a half-wit Watchman to snatch it away from us. Kor! You told me the plan was foolproof!'

The Minister of Intelligence remained calm, except for a telltale glistening of perspiration on his bullet-shaped dome. 'It was foolproof, until . . .'

'Until? Until? I want the Acquataine Cluster, not excuses!'

'And you shall have it,' Marshal Lugal promised. 'As soon as the army is re-equipped and . . .'

'As soon as! Until!' Kanus' voice rose to a scream. 'We had a plan of conquest and it failed. I should have the lot of you thrown to the dogs! And you, Kor; this was your operation, your plan. You picked this mind reader ... Odal. He was to be the express instrument of my will. And he *failed*! You both failed. Twice! Can you give me any reason for allowing you to continue to pollute the air with your presence?'

Kor replied evenly, 'The Acquataine government is still very shaky and ripe for plucking. Men sympathetic to you, my Leader, have gained important posts in that government. Moreover, despite the failures of Major Odal, we are now on the verge of perfecting a new secret weapon, a weapon so powerful that ...'

'A secret weapon?' Kanus' eyes lit up.

Kor lowered his voice a notch. 'It may be possible, our scientists believe, to use a telepath such as Odal and the dueling machine to transport objects from one place to another – over any distance, almost instantaneously.'

Kanus sat silent for a moment, digesting the information. Then he asked:

'Whole armies?'

'Yes.'

'Anywhere in the galaxy?'

'Wherever there is a dueling machine.'

Kanus rose slowly, dramatically, from his chair and stepped over to the huge star map that spanned one entire wall of the spacious room. He swept the whole map with an all-inclusive gesture and shouted:

'Anywhere! I can strike anywhere. And they will never know what hit them!'

He literally danced for joy, prancing back and forth before the map. 'Nothing can stand in our way now! The Terran Commonwealth will fall before us. The galaxy is ours. We will make them tremble at the thought of us. We will make them cower at the mention of my name!'

The men of the Inner Cabinet nodded and murmured agreement.

Suddenly Kanus' face hardened again and he whirled

around to Kor. 'Is this really a secret, or is someone else work-ing on it too? What of this Leoh?'

'It is possible,' Kor replied as blandly as he could, 'that Professor Leoh is also working along the same lines. After all, the dueling machine is his invention. But he does not have the services of a trained telepath, such as Odal.'

Kanus said, 'I do not like the fact that you are depending on this failure, Odal.'

Kor allowed a vicious smile to crack his face. 'We are not depending on him, my Leader. We are using his brain. He is an experimental animal, nothing more.'

Kanus smiled back at the Minister. 'He is not enjoying his new duties, I trust.'

'Hardly,' Kor said.

'Good. Let me see tapes of his ... ah, experiments.'

'With pleasure, my Leader.'

The door to the far end of the room opened and Romis, Minister of Foreign Affairs, stepped in. The room fell into a tense silence as his shoes clicked across the marble floor. Tall, spare, utterly precise, Romis walked straight to the Leader, holding a lengthy report in his hand. His patrician face was graven.

'I have unpleasant news, Chancellor.'

They stood confronting each other, and everyone in the room could see their mutual hatred. Kanus – short, spare, dark – glared up at the silver-hair aristocrat.

'Our embassy in Acquatainia,' Romis continued icily, 're-ports that Sir Harold Spencer has requested permission to base a Star Watch survey expedition temporarily on one of the frontier stars of the Acquaine Cluster. A star near our border, of course. Martine has agreed to it.'

Kanus went white, then his face slowly turned red. He snatched the report from Romis' hand, scanned it, crumpled it, and threw it to the floor. For a few moments he could not even speak. Then the tirade began.

An hour and a half later, when the Leader was once again

coherent enough to speak rationally, his ministers were assuring him:

'The Terrans will only be there temporarily.'

'It's only a small fleet . . . no military value at all.'

'It's a feeble attempt by Martine and Spencer . . .'

At the mention of Spencer's name, Kanus broke into another half-hour of screaming tantrum. Finally, he abruptly stopped.

'Romis! Stop staring out the window and give me your assessment of this situation.'

The Foreign Minister turned slowly from the window and answered, 'You must assume that the Terrans will remain in Acquatainia indefinitely. If they do not, all to the good. But your plans must be based on the assumption that they will. That means you cannot attack Acquatainia by military force . . .'

'Why not?' Kanus demanded.

Romis explained, 'Because the Terrans will immediately become involved in the fighting. The entire Star Watch will be mobilized, under the pretext of saving their survey fleet from danger, as soon as we attack. The fleet is simply an excuse for the Terrans to step in against us.'

But Kanus' eyes began to glow. 'I have the plan,' he announced. Turning to Kor:

'You must push the development of this instantaneous transporter to the ultimate. I want a working device *immediately*. Do you understand?'

'Yes, my Leader.'

Rubbing his hands together joyfully, Kanus said, 'We will have our army appear in the Acquatainian capital. We'll conquer the Cluster from within! Wherever they have a dueling machine, we'll appear and conquer with the swiftness of lightning! Let the Star Watch plant their hostages on the frontier . . . they'll gather cobwebs there! We'll have the whole Cluster in our fist before Spencer even realizes we've moved!'

Kanus laughed uproariously, and all his aides laughed with him.

All except Romis.

*

Professor Leoh slouched unhappily in a chair at the dueling machine's main control desk. Hector sat uneasily on the first few centimeters of the desk edge.

'We have adequate power,' Leoh said, 'the circuits are correct, everything seems normal.' He looked up, puzzled, at Hector.

The Watchman stammered, 'I know . . . I just . . . well, I just can't do it.'

Shaking his head Leoh said, 'We've duplicated the conditions of your first jump. But now it doesn't work. If the machine is exactly the same, then there must be something different about you.'

Hector wormed his shoulders uncomfortably.

'What is it, my boy? What's bothering you? You haven't been yourself since the night you caught Odal.'

Hector didn't reply.

'Listen,' said Leoh. 'Psychic phenomena are very difficult to pin down. For centuries men have known cases where people have apparently teleported, or used telepathy. There are thousands of cases on record of poltergeists – they were actually thought to be ghosts, ages ago. Now I'm sure that they're really cases of telekinesis: the poltergeist was actually a fairly normal human being, under extraordinary stress, who threw objects around his house mentally without even knowing it himself.'

'Just like when I jumped without knowing it,' Hector said.

'Exactly. Now, it was my hope that the dueling machine would amplify the psychic talent in you. It did once, but it's not doing it now.'

'Maybe I don't really have it.'

'Maybe,' Leoh admitted. Then, leaning forward in his chair

and pointing a stubby finger at the Watchman, he added, 'Or maybe something's upsetting you so much that your talent is buried, dormant, switched off.'

'Yes ... well, uh, that is ...'

'Is it Geri? I haven't seen her around here lately. Perhaps if she could come ... after all, she was one of the conditions of your original jump, wasn't she?'

'She won't come here,' Hector said miserably.

'Eh? Why not?'

The Watchman blurted, 'Because she wanted me to murder Odal and I wouldn't, so she's sore at me and won't even talk to me on the view phone.'

'What? What's this? Take it slower, son.'

Hector explained the whole story of Geri's insistence that Odal be killed.

Leaning back in the chair, fingers steepled on his broad girth, Leoh said, 'Hmm. Natural enough, I suppose. The Acquatainians have that sort of outlook. But somehow I expected better of her.'

'She won't even talk to me,' Hector repeated.

'But you did the right thing,' said Leoh. 'At least, you were true to your upbringing and your Star Watch training. Vengeance is a paltry motive, and nothing except self-defense can possibly justify killing a man.'

'Tell it to her.'

'No, my boy,' Leoh said, pulling himself up and out of the chair. 'You must tell her. And in no uncertain terms.'

'But she won't even see me ...'

'Nonsense. If you love her, you'll get to her. Tell her where you stand and why. If she loves you, she'll accept you for what you are, and be proud of you for it.'

Hector looked uncertain. 'And if she doesn't love me?'

'Well ... knowing the Acquatainian temperament, she might start throwing things at you.'

The Watchman remained sitting on the desk top and stared down at the floor.

Leoh grasped his shoulder. 'Listen to me, son. What you did took courage, real courage. It would have been easy to kill Odal and win her approval ... everyone's approval, as a matter of fact. But you did what you thought was right. Now, if you had the courage to do that, surely you have the courage to face an unarmed girl.'

Hector looked up at him, his long face somber. 'But suppose ... suppose she never loved me. Suppose she was just ... well, *using* me ... until I killed Odal?'

Then you're well rid of her, Leoh thought. But he couldn't say that to Hector.

'I don't think that's the case at all,' he said softly.

And he added to himself, At *least I hope not*.

*

In his exhausted sleep, Odal did not hear the door opening. The sergeant stepped into the bare windowless cell and shined his lamp in Odal's eyes. The Kerak major stirred and turned his face away from the light. The sergeant grabbed his shoulder and shook him sternly.

Odal snapped awake, knocked the guard's hand from his shoulder, and seized him by the throat. The guard dropped his lamp and tried to pry Odal's single hand from his windpipe. For a second or two they remained locked in soundless fury, in the weird glow from the lamp on the floor – Odal sitting up on the cot, the sergeant slowly sinking to his knees.

Then Odal released him. The sergeant fell to all fours, coughing. Odal swung his legs out of the cot and stood up.

'When you rouse me, you will do it with courtesy,' he said. 'I am not a common criminal, and I will not be treated as one by such as you. And even though my door is locked from the outside, you will knock on it before entering. Is that clear?'

The sergeant climbed to his feet, rubbing his throat, his eyes a mixture of anger and fear.

'I'm just following orders. Nobody told me to treat you special ...'

'I am telling you,' Odal snapped. 'And as long as I still have my rank, you will address me as *sir*!'

'Yes, sir,' the sergeant muttered sullenly.

Odal relaxed slightly, flexed his fingers.

'You're wanted at the dueling machine . . . sir.'

'In the middle of the night? By whose orders?'

The guard shrugged. 'They didn't say. Sir.'

Odal smiled. 'Very well. Step outside while I put on my "uniform."' He gestured to the shapeless fatigues draped over the end of the cot.

A single meditech stood waiting for Odal beside the dueling machine, which bulked ominously in the dim night lighting. Odal recognized him as one of the inquisitors he had been facing for the past several weeks. Wordlessly, the man gestured Odal to his booth. The sergeant took up a post at the doorway to the large room as the meditech fitted Odal's head and torso with the necessary neurocontacts. Then he stepped out of the compartment and firmly shut the door.

For a few moments nothing happened. Then Odal felt a voice in his mind:

'Major Odal?'

'Of course,' he replied silently.

'Yes . . . of course.'

There was something puzzling. Something wrong. 'You . . . you are not the . . .'

'I am not the man who put you into the dueling machine. That is correct.' The voice seemed both pleased and worried. 'That man is at the controls of the machine, while I am halfway across the planet. He has a miniature transceiver with him, and I am communicating with you through it. This means of communication is unorthodox, but it probably cannot be intercepted by Kor or his henchmen.'

'But I know you,' Odal thought. 'I have met you before.'

'That is true.'

'Romis! You are Minister Romis.'

'Yes.'

'What do you want with me?'

'I learned only this morning of your situation. I was shocked at such treatment for a loyal soldier of Kerak.'

Odal felt the words forming in his mind, yet he knew that Romis' words were only a glossy surface, hiding a deeper meaning. He communicated nothing, and waited for the Minister to continue.

'Are you being mistreated?'

Odal smiled mirthlessly. 'No more so than any laboratory animal. I suppose it's no worse than having one's intestines sliced open without anesthetics.'

Romis' mind recoiled. Then he recovered and said, 'There might be some way in which I can help you ...'

Odal lost his patience. 'You haven't contacted me in the middle of the night, using this elaborate procedure, to ask about my comfort. Something is troubling you greatly and you believe I can be useful to you.'

'Can you actually read my thoughts?'

'Not in the manner one reads a tape. But I can sense things ... and the dueling machine amplifies this talent.'

Romis hesitated a moment, then asked, 'Can you ... sense ... what is in my mind?'

Now it was Odal's turn to hesitate. Was this a trap? He glanced around the confining walls of the tiny booth, and at the door that he knew was locked from the outside. *What more can they do? Kill me?*

'I can feel in your thoughts,' Odal replied, 'a hatred for Kanus. A hatred that is matched only by your fear of him. If you had it in your power you would ...'

'I would what?'

Odal finally saw the picture clearly. 'You would have the Leader assassinated.'

'How?'

'By a disgraced army officer who would have good cause to hate Kanus.'

'You have cause to hate him,' Romis emphasized.

'Perhaps.'

'Perhaps? Can you fail to hate him?'

Odal shook his head. 'I've never considered the question. He is the Leader. I have neither loved nor hated, only followed his commands.'

'Duty above self,' Romis' thought returned. 'You speak like a member of the nobility.'

'Such as you are. And yet you wish to assassinate the Leader.'

'Yes! Because a true member of the nobility puts his duty to the Kerak Worlds before his allegiance to this madman – this usurper of power who will destroy us all, nobleman and commoner alike.'

'I am only a commoner,' Odal replied, very deliberately. 'Perhaps I'm not equipped to decide where my duty lies. Certainly, I have no choice in my duties at present.'

Romis recovered his composure. 'Listen to me. If you agree to join us, we can help you escape from this beastly experimentation. As you can see, certain members of Kor's staff are with us; so too are groups in the army and space fleet. If you will help us, you can once again be a hero of Kerak.'

If I murder Kanus and survive the deed, Odal thought to himself. *And if I am not then assassinated in turn by your friends.*

To Romis he asked, 'And if I don't agree to join you?'

The Minister remained silent.

'I see,' Odal answered for himself. 'I know too much now to be allowed the risk of living.'

'Unfortunately the stakes are too high to let personal feelings intervene. If you do not agree to help us before leaving the dueling machine, the medical technician and sergeant are waiting outside for you. They have their orders.'

'To murder me,' Odal said bluntly, 'and make it seem as though I tried to escape.'

'Yes. I am sorry to be brutal, but that is your choice. Join or die.'

*

While Odal deliberated his choice in the midnight darkness of Kerak, it was sunset in the capital city of Acquatainia.

High above the city, Hector circled warily in a rented air car that had been ready for the junk heap long ago. He kept his eyes riveted to the view screen on the control panel in front of him, sitting tensely in the pilot's seat; the four-place cabin was otherwise empty.

Part of his circle carried him through one of the city's busier traffic patterns, but he ignored other air cars and kept the autopilot locked on its circle while homeward-bound commuters shrieked into their radios at him and dodged around the Watchman's vehicle. Hector had his radio off; every nerve in his body was concentrating on the view screens.

The car's tri-di scanners were centered on Geri Dulaq's house, on the outskirts of the city. As far as Hector was concerned, nothing else existed. Cars buzzed by his bubble-topped canopy and apoplectic-faced drivers shook their fists at him. He never saw them. Wind whistled suspiciously through what should have been a sealed cabin; the air car groaned and rattled when it should have hummed and soared. He never noticed.

There she is! He felt a charge of electricity flash through him as he saw her at last, walking through the garden next to the house.

For an instant he wondered if he had the nerve to go through with it, but his hands had already nudged the controls and the air car, shuddering, started a long whining descent toward the house.

The reddish sun of Acquatainia was shining straight into Hector's eyes, through the ancient photochromic canopy that was supposed to screen out the glare. Squinting hard, Hector barely made out the menacing bulk of the house as it rose to meet him. He pulled back on the controls, jammed the brake flaps full open, flipped the screeching engine pods to their landing angle, and bounced the car in a shower of dust and noise and wind squarely into Geri's flower bed.

'*You!*' she screamed as he popped the canopy open.

She turned and ran to the house. He went to leap out after her, but the seat harness yanked cuttingly at his middle and shoulders.

By the time Hector had unbuckled the harness and jumped, stumbling, to the ground, she was inside the house. But the door was still open, he saw. Hector sprinted toward it.

A servant, rather elderly, appeared on the walk before the door. Hector ducked under his feebly waving arms and launched himself toward the door, which was now swinging shut. He got halfway through before the door slammed against him, wedging him firmly against the jamb.

Hector could hear someone panting behind the door, struggling to get it closed despite the fact that one of his arms and a leg were flailing inside the doorway. Hoping it wasn't Geri, he pushed hard against the door. It hardly budged. *It's not her*, he realized. Setting himself as solidly as he could on his outside leg, he pushed with all his might. The door gave slowly, then suddenly burst open. Hector sailed off balance into the husky servant who had been pushing against him. They both sprawled onto the hard plastiwood floor of the entryway.

Hector groped to all fours and caught a glimpse of Geri at the top of the wide, curving stairway that dominated the main hall of the house. Then the servant fell on him and tried to pin him down. He rolled over on top of the servant, broke loose from his clumsy grip, and got to his feet.

'I don't want to hurt you!' he said shakily, holding his hands out in what he hoped was a menacing position. Another pair of arms grappled at him from behind, but weakly. The old servant. Hector shrugged him off and took a few more steps into the house, his eyes still on the husky one, who was now crouched on the floor and looking up questioningly at Geri.

All she has to do is nod, Hector knew, *and they'll both jump me.*

'I told you I never wanted to see you again!' she screamed at him. 'Never!'

'I've got to talk to you,' he shouted back. 'Just for five minutes . . . Uh, alone.'

'I don't . . . your nose is bleeding.'

He touched his upper lip with a finger. It came away red and sticky.

'Oh . . . the door . . . I must've banged it on the door.'

Geri took a few steps down the stairway, hesitated, then seemed to take a deep breath and came slowly down the rest of the way.

'It's all right,' she said calmly to the servants. 'You may leave.'

The brawny one looked uncertain. The old one piped, 'But if he . . .'

'I'll be all right,' Geri insisted firmly. 'You can stay in the next room, if you like. The Lieutenant will only be here for five minutes. No longer,' she added, turning to Hector.

They withdrew reluctantly.

'You ruined my flowers,' she said to Hector. But softly, and the corners of her mouth looked as though they wanted to turn up. 'And your nose is still bleeding.'

Hector fumbled through his pockets. She produced a tissue from a pocket in her dress.

'Here. Now clean yourself up and leave.'

'Not until I've said what I came to say,' Hector replied nasally, holding the tissue against his nose.

'Keep your head up, don't bleed on the floor.'

'It's hard to talk like this.'

Despite herself, Geri smiled. 'Well, it's your own fault. You can't come swooping into people's gardens like . . . like . . .'

'You wouldn't see me. And I had to tell you.'

'Tell me what?'

162

Putting his head down, his neck cracking painfully as he did, Hector said:

'Well . . . blast it, Geri, I love you. But I'm not going to be your hired assassin. And if you loved me, you wouldn't want me to be. A man's not supposed to be a trained pet . . . to do whatever his girl wants him to. I'm not . . .'

Her expression hardened. 'I only asked you to do what I would have done myself, if I could have.'

'You would've killed Odal?'

'Yes.'

'Because he murdered your father.'

'That's right.'

Hector took the tissue away from his face. 'But Odal was just following orders. Kanus is the one who ordered your father killed.'

'Then I'd kill Kanus, too, if I had the chance,' she snapped angrily.

'You'd kill anybody who had a hand in your father's death?'

'Of course.'

'The other soldiers, the ones who helped Odal during the duel, you'd kill them too?'

'Certainly!'

'Anybody who helped Odal? Anybody at all? The starship crew that brought him here?'

'Yes! All of them! Anybody!'

Hector put his hand out slowly and took her by the shoulder. 'Then you'd have to kill me, too, because I let him go. I helped him to escape from you.'

She started to answer. Her mouth opened. Then her eyes filled with tears and she leaned against Hector and began crying.

He put his arms around her. 'It's all right, Geri. It's all right. I know how much it hurts. But . . . you can't expect me to be just as much of a murderer as he is . . . I mean, well, it's just not the way to . . .'

'I know,' she said, still sobbing. 'I know, Hector. I know.'

For a few moments they remained there, holding each other. Then she looked up at him, and he kissed her.

'I've missed you,' she said, very softly.

He felt himself grinning like a circus clown. 'I . . . well, I've missed you, too.'

They laughed together, and she pulled out another tissue and dabbed at his nose with it.

'I'm sorry about the flowers.'

'That's all right, they'll . . .' She stopped and stared toward the doorway.

Turning, Hector saw a blue-anodized robot, about the size and shape of an upended cargo crate, buzzing officiously at the open doorway. Its single photoeye seemed to brighten at the sight of his face.

'You are Star Watch Lieutenant Hector H. Hector, the operator of the vehicle parked in the flower bed?' it inquired tinnily.

Hector nodded dumbly.

'Charges have been lodged against you, sir: violations of flight safety regulation regarding use of traffic lanes, failure to acknowledge radio intercept, unauthorized flight patterns, failure to maintain minimum altitude over a residential zone, landing in an unauthorized area, trespass, illegal and violent entry into a private domicile, assault and battery. You are advised to refrain from making any statement until you obtain counsel. You will come with me, or additional charges of resisting arrest will be lodged against you. Thank you.'

The Watchman sagged; his shoulders slumped dejectedly.

Geri barely suppressed a giggle. 'It's all right, Hector. I'll get a lawyer. If they send you to jail, I'll visit you. It'll be very romantic.'

*

Odal sat in the darkness of the dueling machine booth, turning thoughts over and over in his mind. To remain as Kor's experimental animal meant disgrace and the torture of ceaseless mind-probing. Ultimately an utterly unpleasant death. To join Romis meant an attempt to assassinate the Leader; an attempt that would end, successful or not, in death at the hands of Kanus' guards. To refuse to join Romis led again – and this time immediately – to death.

Every avenue of choice came to the same end. Odal sat there calmly and examined his alternatives with a cool detachment, almost as though this was happening to someone else. It was even amusing, almost, that events could arrange themselves so overwhelmingly against a lone man.

Romis' voice in his mind was imperative. 'I cannot keep this link open much longer without risking detection. What is your decision?'

To stay alive as long as possible, Odal realized. Hoping that thought didn't get across to Romis, he said, 'I'll join you.'

'You do this willingly?'

A picture of the armed guard waiting for him outside flashed through Odal's mind. 'Yes, willingly,' he said. 'Of course.'

'Very well, then. Remain where you are, act as though nothing has happened. Within the next few days, a week at most, we'll get you out of Kor's hands.'

Only when he was certain that contact was broken, that Romis and the relay man at the machine's controls could no longer hear him, did Odal allow himself to think: *If I round up Romis and all the plotters against the Leader, that should make me a hero of Kerak again.*

Hector was all smiles as he strode into the dueling machine chamber. Geri was on his arm, also smiling.

Leoh said pleasantly, 'Well, now that you're together again and you've paid all your traffic fines, I hope you're emotionally prepared to go to work.'

'Just watch me,' said Hector.

They began slowly. First Hector merely teleported himself from one booth of the dueling machine to the other. He did it a dozen times the first day. Leoh measured the transit time and the power drain each time. It took four picoseconds, on the average, to make the jump. And – according to the desk-top calculator Leoh had set up alongside the control panels – the power drain was approximately equal to that of a star ship's drive engines pushing a mass equal to Hector's weight.

'Do you realize what this means?' he asked of them.

Hector was perched on the desk top again, with Geri sitting in a chair she had pulled up beside Leoh's. Drumming his fingers thoughtfully on the control panel for a moment, Hector replied, 'Well . . . it means we can move things about as efficiently as a star ship . . .'

'Not quite,' Leoh corrected. 'We can move things or people as efficiently as a star ship moves its *payload*. We needn't lift a star ship's structure or power drive. Our drive – the dueling machine – can remain on the ground. Only the payload is transported.'

'Can you go as fast as a star ship?' Geri asked.

'Seemingly faster, if these tests mean anything,' Leoh answered.

'Am I traveling in subspace,' Hector wanted to know, 'like a star ship does? Or what?'

'Probably "what," I'd guess,' said Leoh. 'But it's only a guess. We have no idea of how this works, how fast you can really go, how far you can teleport, or any of the limits of the phenomenon. There's a mountain of work to do.'

For the next few days, Hector moved inanimate objects while he sat on one booth of the dueling machine. He lifted weights without touching them, and then even transported Geri from one booth to the other. But he could only move things inside the dueling machine.

'We may have an interstellar transport mechanism here,' Leoh said at the end of a week, tired but enormously happy. 'There'd have to be a dueling machine, or something like it, at the other end, though.'

The pain was unbearable. Odal screamed soundlessly, in

166

his mind, as a dozen lances of fire drilled through him. His body jerked spasmodically, arms and legs twitching uncontrolled, innards cramping and coiling, heart pounding dangerously fast. He couldn't see, couldn't hear, could only taste blood in his mouth.

Romis! Where is Romis? Why doesn't he come? He would have told his inquistors everything, anything, just to make them stop. But they weren't even asking him questions. They weren't interested in his memories or his confessions.

JUMP!

Transport yourself to the next booth.

You are a trained telepath, you must have latent teleportation powers, as well.

We will not ease up on this pressure until you teleport to the next booth. Indeed, the pressure will be increased until you do as you are told.

JUMP!

Hector sat in the dueling machine in Acquatainia and concentrated on his job. A drawerful of papers, tapes, and holograms was in the other booth. Hector was going to transport it to a dueling machine on the other side of the planet. This would be the first long-distance jump.

It wasn't easy to concentrate. Geri was waiting for him outside. Leoh had been working him all day. A stray thought of Odal crossed his mind: *I wonder what he's up to now? Is he working on teleportation too?*

He felt a brief tingling sensation, like a mild electric shock. 'Funny,' he muttered.

Puzzled, he removed the neurocontacts from his head and body, got up, and opened the booth door.

The technicians at the control desk gaped at him. It took Hector a full five seconds to realize that they were wearing Kerak uniforms. A pair of guards, looking equally startled, reached for their side arms as soon as they recognized the Star Watch emblem on Hector's cover-alls.

He had time to say, 'Oh-oh,' before the guards shot him down.

On Acquatainia, Leoh was shaking his head unhappily as he inspected the pile of materials that Hector was supposed to teleport.

'Nothing,' he muttered. 'It didn't work at all.'

His puzzled musing was shattered by Geri's scream. Looking up, he saw her cowering against the control desk, screaming in uncontrolled hysteria. Framed in the doorway of the farther booth stood the tall, lithe figure of Odal.

*

'This is absolutely fantastic,' said Sir Harold Spencer.

Leoh nodded agreement. The old scientist was at his desk in the office behind the dueling machine chamber. Spencer seemed to be on a star ship, from the looks of the austere, metal-walled cabin that was visible behind his tri-di image.

'He actually jumped from Kerak to Acquatainia?' Spencer still looked unconvinced.

'In something less than a second,' Leoh repeated. 'Four hundred and fifty light years in less than a second.'

Spencer's brow darkened. 'Do you realize what you've done, Albert? The military potential of this ... teleportation. And Kanus must know all about it, too.'

'Yes. And he's holding Hector somewhere in Kerak. We've got to get him out ... if he's still alive.'

'I know,' Spencer said, absolutely glowering now. 'And what about this Kerak assassin? I suppose the Acquatainians have him safely filed away?'

Nodding again, Leoh answered, 'They're not quite sure what to do with him. Technically, he's not charged with any crimes. Actually, the last thing in the world anyone wants is to send him back to Kerak.'

'Why did he leave? Why come back to Acquatainia?'

'Don't know. Odal won't tell us anything, except to claim

asylum on Acquatainia. Most people here think it's another sort of trick.'

Spencer drummed his fingers on his thigh impatiently. 'So Odal is imprisoned in Acquatainia, Hector is presumably jailed in Kerak – or worse. And I have a survey fleet heading for the Acquataine-Kerak frontier on a mission that's now obviously hopeless. Kanus needn't fight his way into Acquatainia. He can pop into the midst of the Cluster, wherever there are dueling machines.'

'We could shut them down, or guard them,' Leoh suggested.

Frowning again, Spencer pointed out, 'There's nothing to prevent Kanus from building machines inside every Kerak embassy or consulate building in the Cluster ... or in the Commonwealth, for that matter. Nothing short of war can stop him from doing that.'

'And war is exactly what we're trying to prevent.'

'We've got to prevent it,' Spencer rumbled, 'if we want to keep the Commonwealth intact.'

Now Leoh was starting to feel as gloomy as Sir Harold. 'And Hector? What about him? We can't abandon him ... Kanus could kill him.'

'I know. I'll call Romis, the Foreign Minister. Of that whole lot around Kanus, he's the only one who seems capable of telling the truth.'

'What can you do if they refuse to return Hector?'

'They'll probably offer to trade him for Odal.'

'But Odal doesn't want to go,' Leoh said. 'And the Acquatainians might not surrender him. If they hold Odal and Kanus keeps Hector, then the Commonwealth will be forced into ...'

'Into threatening Kerak with armed force if they don't release Hector. Good Lord, this lieutenant could trigger off the war we're trying to avert!'

Spencer looked as appalled as Leoh felt.

*

Minister Romis left his country villa punctually at dawn for his usual morning ride. He proceeded along the bridle path, however, only until he was out of sight of the villa and any possible spies of Kor's. Then he turned his mount off the path and into the thick woods. After a hard climb upslope, he came to a little clearing atop a knoll.

Standing in the clearing was a small shuttle craft, its hatch flanked by a pair of armed guards. Wordlessly, Romis dismounted and went into the craft. A man dressed identically, and about the same height and build as the Foreign Minister, came out and mounted the animal and continued the ride.

Within moments, the shuttle craft rose on muffled jets and hurtled up and out of Kerak's atmosphere. Romis entered the control compartment and sat beside the pilot.

'This is a risky business, sir,' the pilot said. 'We could be spotted from the ground.'

'The nearest tracking station is manned by friends of ours,' Romis said tiredly. 'At least, they were friends the last time I talked with them. One must take some risks in an enterprise of this sort, and the chief risk seems to be friends who change sides.'

The pilot nodded unhappily. Twelve minutes after lift-off the shuttle craft made rendezvous with an orbiting star ship that bore the insignia of the Kerak space fleet. A craggy-faced captain met Romis at the air lock and guided him down a narrow passageway to a small, guarded compartment. They stepped in. Lying on the bunk built into the compartment's curving outer bulkhead was the inert form of Star Watch Lieutenant Hector. Nearby sat one of the guards and a medi-tech who had been at the dueling machine. They rose and stood at attention.

'None of Kor's people know about him?' Romis' voice was quiet, but urgent.

'No, sir,' said the meditech. 'The interrogators were all

knocked unconscious by the power surge when Major Odal and the Watchman transferred with each other. We were able to get the Watchman here without being detected.'

'Hopefully,' Romis added. Then he asked, 'How is he?'

The meditech replied, 'Sleeping like a child, sir. We thought it best to keep him drugged.'

Romis nodded.

'At my order,' the captain said, 'they've given the Watchman several doses of truth drugs. We've been questioning him. No sense allowing an opportunity like this to go to waste.'

'Quite right,' said Romis. 'What have you learned?'

The captain's face darkened. 'Absolutely nothing. Either he knows nothing ... which is hard to believe, or,' he went on, shifting his gaze to the meditech, 'he can overcome the effects of the drug.'

Shrugging, Romis turned back to the meditech. 'You are certain that you got away from Kor undetected.'

'Yes, sir. We went by the usual route, using only those men we know are loyal to our cause.'

'Good. Now let us pray that none of our loyal friends decide to change loyalties.'

The captain asked, 'How are you going to explain Odal's disappearance? The Leader will be told about it this morning, won't he?'

'That is correct. And I do not intend to say a word. Kor assumes that Odal, and this meditech and guard, all escaped in the dueling machine. Let him continue to assume that; no suspicion will fall on us.'

The captain murmured approval.

There was a rap at the door. The captain opened it, and the guard outside handed him a written message. The captain scanned it, then handed it to Romis, saying, 'Your tri-di link has been set up.'

Romis crumpled the message in his hand. 'I had better hurry, then, before the beam links enough to be traceable. Here,' he handed the rolled-up paper to the meditech, 'destroy this. Personally.'

Romis quickly made his way to another compartment, farther down the passageway, that served as a communications center. When he and the captain entered the compartment, the communications tech rose, saluted, and discreetly stepped out into the passageway.

Romis sat down before the screen and touched a button on the panel at his side. Instantly the screen showed the bulky form of Sir Harold Spencer, sitting at a metal desk, obviously aboard his own star ship.

Spencer's face was a thundercloud. 'Minister Romis. I was going to call you when your call arrived here.'

Romis smiled easily and replied, 'From the expression on your face, Commander, I believe you already know the reason for my calling.'

Sir Harold did not return the smile. 'You are a well-trained diplomat, sir. I am only a soldier. Let's come directly to the point.'

'Of course. A major in the Kerak army has disappeared, and I have reason to believe he is on Acquatainia.'

Spencer huffed. 'And a Star Watch lieutenant has disappeared, and I have reason to believe he is on Kerak.'

'Your suspicions are not without foundation,' Romis fenced coolly. 'And mine?'

The Star Watch Commander rubbed a hand across his massive jaw before answering. 'You have been using the words "I" and "mine" instead of the usual diplomatic plurals. Could it be that you are not speaking on behalf of the Kerak government?'

Romis glanced up at the captain, standing by the door out of camera range; he gave only a worried frown and a gesture to indicate that time was racing.

'It happens,' Romis said to Sir Harold, 'that I am not

speaking for the government at this moment. If you have custody of the missing Kerak major, you can probably learn the details of my position from him.'

'I see,' Spencer said. 'And should I assume that you – and not Kanus and his gang of hoodlums – have custody of Lieutenant Hector?'

Romis nodded.

'You wish to exchange him for Major Odal?'

'No, not at all. The Major is . . . safer . . . where he is, for the time being. We have no desire for his return to Kerak at the moment. Perhaps later. However, we do want to assure you that no harm will come to Lieutenant Hector – no matter what happens here on Kerak.'

Spencer sat wordlessly for several seconds. At length he said, 'You seem to be saying that there will be an upheaval in Kerak's government shortly, and you will hold Lieutenant Hector hostage to make certain that the Star Watch does not interfere. Is that correct?'

'You put it rather bluntly,' Romis said, 'but, in essence, you are correct.'

'Very well,' said Spencer. 'Go ahead and have your upheaval. But let me warn you: if, for any reason whatever, harm should befall a Star Watchman, you will have an invasion on your hands as quickly as star ships can reach your worlds. I will not wait for authorization from the Terran Council or any other formalities. I will crush you, one and all. Is that clear?'

'Quite clear,' Romis replied, his face reddening. 'Quite clear.'

*

Leoh had to make his way through the length of the Acquatainian Justice Department's longest hallway, down a lift tube to a sub-sub-basement, past four checkpoints guarded by a dozen armed and uniformed men each, into an anteroom where another pair of guards sat next to a tri-di scanner, and finally – after being stopped, photographed, questioned, and made to show his special identification card and pass each step of the way – entered Odal's quarters.

It was a comfortable suite of rooms, deep underground, originally built for the Secretary of Justice as a blast shelter during the previous Acquataine-Kerak war.

'You're certainly well guarded,' the old man said to Odal as he entered.

The Kerak major had been sitting on a plush lounge, listening to a music tape. He flicked the music silent and rose as Leoh walked into the room. The outside door clicked shut behind the scientist.

'I'm being protected, they tell me,' said Odal, 'both from the Acquatainian populace and from the Kerak embassy.'

'Are they treating you well?' Leoh asked as he sat, un-invited, on an easy chair next to the lounge.

'Well enough. I have music, tri-di, food and drink.' Odal's voice had a ring of irony in it. 'I'm even allowed to see the sun once a day, when I get my prison-yard exercise.'

As Odal sat back in the lounge, Leoh looked closely at him. He seemed different. No more icy smile and haughty manner. There were lines in his face that had been put there by pain, but not by pain alone. Disillusionment perhaps. The world was no longer his personal arena of triumph. Leoh thought, *He's settled down to the same business that haunts us all: survival.*

Aloud, he said, 'Sir Harold Spencer has been in touch with your Foreign Minister, Romis.'

Odal kept his face blank, noncommittal.

'Harold has asked me to speak with you, to find out where you stand in all of this. The situation is quite confused.'

'It seems simple to me,' Odal said. 'You have me. Romis has Hector.'

'Yes, but where do we go from here? Is Kanus going to attack Acquatainia? Is Romis going to try to overthrow Kanus? Harold has been trying to avert a war, but if anything happens to Hector he'll swoop in with every Star

Watch ship he can muster. And where do you stand? Which side are you on?'

Odal almost smiled. 'I've been asking myself that very question. So far, I haven't been able to find a clear answer.'

'It's important for us to know.'

'Is it?' Odal asked, leaning forward slightly in the lounge. 'Why is that? I'm a prisoner here. I'm not going anywhere.'

'You needn't be a prisoner. I'm sure that Harold and Prime Minister Martine would agree to have you released if you guaranteed to help us.'

'Help you? How?'

'For one thing,' Leoh answered, 'you could help us to get Hector back to safety.'

'Return to Kerak?' Odal tensed. 'That would be risky.'

'You'd rather sit safely here, a prisoner?'

'Why not?'

Leoh shifted his weight uncomfortably in the chair. 'I should think that Romis could use you in his attempt to overthrow Kanus.'

'Possibly. But not until the moment he's ready to strike directly at Kanus. Until then, I imagine he's just as happy to let me remain here. He'll call me when he wants me. Whether I'll go or not is another problem.'

Leoh suddenly found that he had run out of words. It seemed clear that Odal was not going to volunteer to help anyone except himself.

Rising, he said, 'I'd like you to think about these matters. There are many lives at stake, and you could help to save them.'

'And lose my own,' Odal said as he politely stood up.

Leoh cocked his head to one side. 'Very possibly, I must admit.'

'You regard Hector's life more highly than my own. I don't.'

'All right then, stalemate. But there are a few billion Kerak and Acquatainian lives at stake, you know.'

Leoh started for the door. Odal remained standing in front of the lounge. Then he called:

'Professor. That girl . . . the one who was so startled when I arrived at your dueling machine. Who is she?'

Leoh turned. 'Geri Dulaq. The late Prime Minister's daughter.'

'Oh, I see.' For an instant, Odal's nearly expressionless face seemed to show something: disappointment, regret?

'She hates me, doesn't she?' he asked.

'To use your own words,' said Leoh, 'why not?'

*

Hector scratched his head thoughtfully and said, 'This sort of, well, puts me in a . . . um, funny position.'

The Kerak captain shrugged. 'We are all in an extremely delicate position.'

'Well, I suppose so, if . . . that is, I mean . . . how do I know you're telling me the truth?'

The captain's blunt, seamed face hardened angrily for a moment. They were sitting on the bridge of the orbiting star ship to which Hector had been brought. Beyond the protective rail, on the level below, was the control center of the mammoth vessel. The captain controlled his rage and replied evenly:

'A Kerak officer does not tell lies. Under any circumstances. My – superior, let us say – has spoken to the Star Watch Commander, as I explained to you. They reached an agreement whereby you are to remain on this ship until further notice. I am willing to allow you free rein of the ship, exclusive of the control center itself, the power plant, and the air locks. I believe that this is more than fair.'

Hector drummed his fingers on the chart table next to him. 'Guess I've got no choice, really. I'm sort of, well, halfway between a prisoner and, um, a cultural exchange tourist.'

The captain smiled mechanically, trying to ignore the maddening finger-drumming.

'And I'll be staying with you,' Hector went on, 'until you assassinate Kanus.'

'DON'T SAY THAT!' The Captain almost leaped into Hector's lap and clapped a hand over the Watchman's mouth.

'Oh. Doesn't the crew know about it?'

The captain rubbed his forehead with a shaky hand. 'How ... who ... whatever gave you the idea that we would ... contemplate such a thing?'

Hector frowned in puzzlement. 'I don't really know. Just odds and ends. You know. A few things my guards have said. And I figure that Kanus would have pickled my brain by now. You haven't. I'm being treated almost like a guest. So you're not working for Kanus. Yet you're wearing Kerak insignia. Therefore you must be ...'

'Enough! Please, it is not necessary to go into any more detail.'

'Okay.' Hector got to his feet. 'It's all right for me to walk through the ship?'

'Yes; with the exceptions I mentioned.' The captain rose also. 'Oh, yes, there is one other forbidden area: the computers. I understand you were in there this morning.'

Hector nodded. 'The guards let me go in. I was taking my after-breakfast exercise. The guards insisted on it. The exercise, that is.'

'That is irrelevant! You discussed computation methods with one of our junior programers ...'

'Yes. I'm pretty good at math, you see and ...'

'Please! I don't know what you told him, but in attempting to put your so-called "improvements" into the computer program, he blew out three banks of logic circuits and caused a shutdown of the computer for several hours.'

'Oh? That's funny.'

'Funny?' the captain snapped.

'I mean odd.'

'I quite agree. Do not enter the computer area again.'

Hector shrugged. 'Okay. You're the captain.'

The young Star Watchman turned and walked away, leaving the captain seething with frustration. He had not saluted; he had not waited until dismissed by the superior officer; he just slouched off like ... like a civilian! And now he was whistling! Aboard ship! The captain sank back into his chair. That computer programer was only the first casualty, he suddenly realized. *Romis had better act quickly. It is only a matter of time before this Watchman drives us all insane.*

The bridge, Hector found, connected to a series of technical stations, such as the navigation section (idle now that the ship was parked in orbit), the communications center (well guarded) and – most interesting of all – the observation center.

Here Hector found a fair-sized compartment crammed with view screens showing almost every section of the ship's interior, and also looking outside in various directions around the ship. Since they were orbiting Kerak's capital planet, most of the exterior views were turned on the ground below.

Hector soon struck up an acquaintance with the men on duty. Despite the Star Watch emblem on his cover-alls, they seemed to accept him as a fellow-sufferer in the military system, rather than a potential enemy.

'That's the capital city,' one of them pointed out.

Hector nodded, impressed. 'Is that where they have the dueling machine?'

'You mean the one at the Ministry of Intelligence? That's over on the other side of the planet. I'll show it to you when we swing over that way.'

'Thanks,' Hector said. 'I'd like to see it ... very much.'

*

Every morning Odal was taken from his underground suite of rooms to the enclosed courtyard of the Justice building for an hour of sunshine and exercise. Under the cold eyes of the guards he ran endless circles around the courtyard's manicured grass, or did push-ups, knee-bends, sit-ups ... anything to break the monotony and prevent the guards from seeing how miserable and lonely he really felt.

Romis, he thought, is no fool. He won't need me until all his plans are finished, until the actual moment to kill the Leader arrives. What could be better for him than to leave me here, and then offer the Watchman – at precisely the right moment – in trade for me? Spencer will have me shipped back to Kerak, too late to do anything but Romis' bidding.

There were stately, pungent trees lining the four sides of the courtyard, and in the middle a full, wide-spreading wonder with golden, stiff leaves that tinkled like glass chimes, whenever a breeze wafted them. As Odal got up, puffing and hot, from a long set of push-ups, he saw Geri Dulaq sitting on the bench under that tree.

He wiped his brow with a towel and, tossing it over his shoulder, walked slowly to her. He hadn't noticed before how beautiful she was. Her face looked calm, but he could sense that she was working hard to keep control of herself.

'Good morning,' he said evenly.

She nodded but said nothing. Not even a smile or a frown. He gestured toward the bench, and when she nodded again, he sat down beside her.

'You're my second visitor,' said Odal.

'I know,' Geri replied. 'Professor Leoh told me about his visit to you. How you refused to try to help Hector.'

Allowing himself a smile, Odal said, 'I thought that's what you'd be here for.'

She turned to face him. 'You can't leave him in Kerak! If Kanus . . .'

'Hector is with Romis. He's safe enough.'

'For how long?'

'As long as any of us,' Odal said.

'No,' Geri insisted. 'He's a prisoner, and he's in danger.'

'You actually love him?'

179

Her eyes had the glint of tears in them. 'Yes,' she said.

Shaking his head in disbelief, Odal asked, 'How can you love that bumbling, tongue-twisted . . .'

'He's stronger than you are!' Geri flashed. 'And braver. He'd never willingly kill anyone, not even you. He let you live when everyone else on the planet – including me – would have shot you down.'

Odal backed away involuntarily.

'You owe your life to Hector,' she said.

'And now I'm supposed to throw it away to save his.'

'That's right. That would be the decent thing to do. It's what he'd do for you.'

'I doubt that.'

'Of course you do. You don't know what decency is.'

He looked at her, carefully this time, trying to fathom the emotions in her face, her voice.

'Do you hate me?' Odal asked.

Her mouth started to form a *yes*, but she hesitated. 'I should; I have every reason to. I . . . I don't know . . . I want to!'

She got up from the bench and walked rapidly, head down, to the nearest exit from the courtyard. Odal watched her for a moment, then went after her. But the guards stopped him as he neared the door. Geri went on through and disappeared from his sight without ever turning back to look at him.

*

'Cowards!' Romis spat. 'Spineless, weak-kneed old women.'

He was pacing the length of the bookshelf-lined study in his villa, slashing out words as cold and sharp as knife blades. Sitting next to the fireplace, holding an ornate glass in his hand, was the captain of the star ship in which Hector was being held.

'They plot for months on end,' Romis muttered, more to himself than the captain. 'They argue the pettiest details for days. They slither around like snakes, trying to make certain that the plan is absolutely foolproof. But as soon as some danger arises, what do they do?'

The captain raised the glass to his lips.

'They back down!' Romis shouted. 'They place their own rotten little lives ahead of the welfare of the Kerak Worlds. They allow that monster to live, for fear that they might die.'

The captain asked, 'Well, what did you expect of them? You can't force them to be brave. The army leaders, maybe. But they've all been arrested. Whole families. Your politician friends are scared out of their wits by Kor. It's a wonder he hasn't picked you up.'

'He won't,' Romis said, smiling strangely. 'Not until he finds out where Odal is. He fears Odal's return. He knows how well the assassin's been trained.'

'Well, you won't be getting Odal back from Spencer unless you give up the Watchman. And once he goes, you can expect Spencer to hover over us like a vulture.'

'Then what must I do? Kill Kanus myself?'

'You can't.' The captain shook his head.

'Why not? You think I lack . . .'

'My old friend, don't lose sight of your objectives. Kanus is the monster, yes. But he's surrounded by lesser monsters. If you try to kill him, you'll be killed yourself.'

'So?'

'Then who will take over leadership of the government? One of Kanus' underlings, of course. Would you like to see Greber in power? Or Kor?'

Romis visibly shuddered. 'Of course not.'

'Then put the idea of personally performing the execution out of your head. It's suicide.'

'But Kanus must be stopped. I'm certain he means to attack Acquatainia before the month is out.' Romis walked over to the fireplace and stared into the flames. 'I suppose we will have to ask for Odal's return. Even if it means giving back the Watchman and having Spencer poised to invade us.'

'Are you sure?'

'What else can we do? If we can pull off the assassination quickly enough, we can keep Spencer out of Kerak. But if we hesitate much longer, we'll be at war with Acquatainia.'

'We can beat the Acquatainians.'

'I know,' Romis replied. 'But once we do, Kanus will be so popular among the people that we wouldn't dare touch him. And then the madman will attack the Terrans. That will pull the house down on all of us.'

'Hmmm.'

Romis turned to face the captain. 'We must return the Watchman and get Odal back here. At once.'

'Good,' said the captain. 'Frankly, the Watchman has been a royal nuisance aboard my ship. He's disrupting everything.'

'How can one man disrupt an entire star ship?'

The captain took a fast final gulp of his drink. 'You don't know this one man.'

As the captain approached his star ship in his personal shuttle craft, he could sense something was wrong.

It was nothing he could see, but the ship simply did not seem right. His worries were confirmed when the shuttle docked inside one of the giant star ship's air locks. The emergency lights were on, and they were very dim at that. The outer hatch was cranked shut by two spacesuited deck hands, and it took nearly fifteen minutes to bring the lock up to normal air pressure, using the auxiliary air pumps.

'What in the name of all the devils has happened here?' the captain stormed to a cringing junior officer as he stepped out of the shuttle.

'It ... it's the power, sir. The power ... shut off.'

'Shut off?'

The officer swallowed nervously and replied, 'Yessir. All at once ... all through the ship ... no power!'

The captain fumed under his breath for a moment, then snapped, 'Crank the inner hatch open and get me to the bridge.'

The deck hands jumped to it, and in a few minutes the captain, junior officer, and lower ratings had deserted the air lock, leaving the shuttle empty and unguarded.

Out of the pressurized control compartment at the far end of the lock stepped Hector, his thin face wary and serious, but not without the flickerings of a slightly self-satisfied smile.

They should be finding the cause of the power failure in a minute or two, he said to himself. *And as soon as the main lights go on, out I go.*

Hector tiptoed around the lock, making certain adjustments to the temporarily inert air pumps and hatch control unit. Then he climbed into the little shuttle, sealed its hatch, and studied the control panel. *Not too tough . . . I think.*

It had been a ridiculously easy job to cause a power breakdown. All Hector had needed was a little time, so that the guards would begin to allow him to roam certain parts of the ship alone. He had spent long hours in the observation center, learning the layout of the mammoth ship and pinpointing his ultimate objective – the Ministry of Intelligence, where a dueling machine was.

An hour ago, he had taken one of his customary strolls from his quarters to the communications center. His guards, after seeing Hector safely seated among a dozen Kerak technicians, relaxed. Hector waited a while, then casually sauntered over to the stairwell that led down to the switching equipment, on the deck below.

Hector nearly fouled his plan completely by missing the second rung on the metal ladder and plummeting to the deck below. For a long moment he lay on his face, trying to look invisible, or at least dead. Finally he risked a peep up the ladder. No one was coming after him; they hadn't noticed. He was safe, for a few minutes.

He quickly found what he wanted: the leads from the main power plants and the communications antennas. He pulled one of the printed circuit elements from a stand-by console and used it to form a bridge between the power lead connectors and the antenna circuit. While the rules of physics claimed that what he was attempting was impossible, Hector knew from a previous experience on a Star Watch ship (he still shuddered at the memory) exactly what this 'accidental' misconnection would do.

It took about fifteen seconds for the power plants to pump all their energy into the short circuit. The effect was a quiet one : no sparks, no smoke, no explosion. All that happened was that all the lights and motors aboard the ship went off simultaneously. The emergency systems turned on immediately, of course. But in the dim auxiliary lighting, and the confusion of the surprised, bewildered, angry men, it was fairly simple for Hector to make his way along a carefully preplanned route to the main air lock.

Now he sat in the captain's shuttle, waiting for the power to return. The main lights flickered briefly, then turned on to full brightness. The air-lock pumps hummed to life, the outer hatch slid open. Hector nudged the throttle and the shuttle edged out of the air lock and away from the orbiting ship.

The Kerak captain needed about ten minutes to piece together all the information : the deliberate misconnection in the switching equipment; Hector's disappearance; and finally, the unauthorized departure of his personal shuttle.

'He's escaped,' the captain mumbled. 'Escaped. When we were just about to send him back.'

'What shall we do, sir? If the planetary patrols detect the ship, he won't be able to identify himself satisfactorily. They'll blast him !'

The captain's eyes lit up at the thought. But then, 'No. If we lose him, the whole Star Watch will pour into Kerak.' He thought for a moment, then told his aides, 'Have our communications men send out a flight plan to the planetary patrol. Tell them that my shuttle and an auxiliary boat are bringing a contingent of men and officers to the Ministry of Intelligence. And get one of the boats ready for immediate departure. Take your best men. This mess is going to get worse before its gets better.'

*

Odal paced his windowless room endlessly: from the wall screen, around the lounge, past the guarded door to the outside hall, to the bedroom doorway, back again. And again, and again, across the thick carpeting.

He was trying to use his mind as a dispassionate computer, to weigh and count and calculate a hundred different factors. But each factor was different, imponderable, non-numerical. And any one of them could determine the length of Odal's life span.

Kanus, Kor, Romis, Hector, and Geri.

If I returned to Kerak, would Kanus restore me to my full honors? I hold the key to teleportation, to a devastating new way to invade and conquer a nation. Or has Kanus found other psychic talents? Would he regard me as a traitor or a spy? Or worst of all, a failure?

Kor. Odal could report everything he knew about Romis' plot to kill the Leader. Which wasn't much. Kor probably already had that much information and more.

What about Romis? Is he still bent on overthrowing the Leader? Does he still want an assassin?

And the Watchman, that bumbling fool. But a teleporter, and probably as fully talented as Odal himself. *I can impress Leoh and Spencer by rescuing him. It would be risky, but if I do it . . . it will impress the girl, too.*

The girl. Geri Dulaq. Yes, Geri. *She has every reason to hate me, and yet there is something other than hate in her eyes. Fear? Anger? They say that hate is very close to love.*

The view screen chimed, snapping Odal from his chain of thought and pacing. He clapped his hands and the wall dissolved, revealing the bulky form of Leoh sitting at his desk in the dueling machine building. The machine itself was partially visible through the open doorway behind the Professor.

'I thought you should know,' Leoh said without preliminaries, his wrinkled face downcast with worry, 'that Hector
has apparently escaped from Romis' hands. We received a
message from one of Romis' friends in the Kerak embassy that
he's disappeared.'

Odal stood absolutely still in the middle of the room. 'Disappeared? What do you mean?'

Shrugging, Leoh replied, 'According to our information,
Hector was being kept aboard an orbiting star ship. He somehow got off the ship in a shuttle craft, presumably heading
for the Kerak dueling machine. The same one you escaped
from. That's all we know.'

'That machine is in Kor's Ministry of Intelligence,' Odal
heard himself saying calmly. But his mind was racing: *Kor,
Hector, Romis, Geri.* 'He's walking straight into the fire.'

'You're the only one who can help him now,' Leoh said.

*Geri. The look on her face. Her voice: 'You wouldn't know
what decency is.'*

'Very well,' said Odal. 'I'll try.'

He had expected to feel either an excitement at the thought
of pleasing Geri, or a new burden of fear at the prospect of
returning to Kor's hands. Instead he felt neither. Nothing.
His emotions seemed turned off – or, perhaps, they were
merely waiting for something to happen.

It was late at night when Odal, closely guarded, arrived
at the dueling machine. He was wearing black from his
throat to his boots, and looked like a grim shadow against the
antiseptic white of the chamber.

Leoh met him at the control desk. The Acquatainian guards
stood back.

'I'm sorry it took so long to get you here. Every minute's
delay could mean Hector's life. And yours.'

Odal smiled tightly at the afterthought.

The old man continued, 'I had to talk to Martine for two
whole hours before he'd permit your release. And I roused
Sir Harold from his sleep. He was less than happy.'

'If I recall the time differential correctly,' Odal said 'it's nearly dawn at Kor's headquarters. An ideal time to arrive.'

'But is their dueling machine on?' Leoh asked. 'We can't make the jump unless the machine on the receiving end is under power.'

Odal thought a moment. 'It might be. When Kor was ... experimenting with me, they used the machine early each morning. It was always turned up to full power when I arrived for the day's testing. They probably turn it on at dawn as a matter of routine.'

'There's one way to find out,' said Leoh, gesturing to the dueling machine.

Odal nodded. The moment had come. He was returning to Kerak. *To what fate? Death or glory? To which allegiance? Kor or Romis? Kill Hector or save him?*

And the picture he held in his mind as they adjusted the neurocontacts and left him in the dueling machine's booth was the picture of Geri's face. He tried to imagine how she would look smiling.

*

It was late at night, dark and wind swept, when Hector skidded the stolen shuttle craft to a bone-rattling stop deep in a ravine a few kilometers from the Intelligence Ministry.

He had come in low and fast, hoping to avoid detection by Kerak scanners. Now, as he stood atop the dented shuttle craft, feeling the wind, hearing its keening through the dark trees in the ravine, he focused his gaze on the beetling towers of the Intelligence building, silhouetted darkly atop a hill against the star-bright sky.

Looks like an ancient castle, Hector thought, without knowing that it was.

He ducked back through the hatch into the equipment storage racks, pulled out a jet belt, and squirmed into it. Then he went forward to the pilot's compartment and turned off all the power on the ship.

Might need her again, in case I can't get to the dueling machine.

It took him ten minutes to grope his way back to the hatch in darkness. Ten minutes, three skin-barkings, and one head-banging of near concussion magnitude. But finally Hector stood outside the hatch once more. He took a deep breath, faced the Intelligence building, and touched the control stud of the jet belt.

In the quiet night, the noise was shattering. Hector's ears rang as he flew, squinting into the stinging wind, toward the castle. *Maybe this isn't the best way to sneak up on them,* he suspected. But now the battlements were looming before him, racing up fast. Cutting power, he tumbled down and hit hard, sprawling on the squared-off top of the tallest tower.

Shaking his head to clear it and get rid of the ear-ringing, Hector got to his feet. He was unhurt. The platform was about ten meters square, with a stairway leading down from one corner. *Did they hear me coming?*

As if in answer, he heard footsteps ticking up the stone stairway. Shrugging off the jet belt, he hefted its weight in his hands, then hurried over to the top of the stairs. A man's head came into view. He turned as he ran up the last few steps and started to whisper hoarsely, 'Are you here, Watchman? I ...'

Hector knocked him unconscious with the jet belt before he could say any more. As he struggled into the Kerak guard's uniform, pulling it over his own cover-alls, Hector suddenly wondered: *How did he know it was a Watchman? Maybe he's been alerted by the star-ship captain. If that's the case, then these people are against Kanus.*

Once inside the guard uniform, Hector started down the steps. Three more guards were waiting for him at the bottom of the flight, in a stone-faced hallway that curved off into darkness. The lighting wasn't very good, but Hector could see that these men were big, tough-looking, and armed with pistols. He hoped they wouldn't notice that he wasn't the same man who had gone up the stairs a few minutes earlier.

Hector grinned at them and fluttered a wave. He kept walking, trying to get past them and down the corridor.

'Hey, you're the . . .' one of the guards started to say, in the Kerak language.

Hector suddenly felt sick. He could barely understand the Kerak tongue, much less speak it. He kept his grin, weak though it was, and walked a bit faster.

The second guard grabbed the first one's arm and cut him short. 'Let him through,' he whispered. 'We'll try to get the word to our people downstairs and get him into the dueling machine and out of here. But don't get caught near him by Kor's people! Understand?'

'All right, but somebody better cut off the scanners that watch the halls.'

'Can't do that without running the risk of alerting Kor himself!'

'We'll have to chance it . . . otherwise they'll spot him in a minute, in a guard uniform four sizes too small for him.'

Hector was past them now, wondering what the whispering was about, but still moving. As he rounded the corner of the corridor, he saw an open lift tube, looking raw and new in the warm polished stone of the wall. The tube was lit and operating. Hector stepped in, said, 'Dueling machine level' in basic Terran to the simple-minded computer that ran the tube, and closed his eyes.

The computer's squeaky voice echoed back, 'Dueling machine level; turn left, then right.' Hector opened his eyes and stepped out of the tube. The corridor here was much brighter, better lit. But there was still no one in sight.

It was almost like magic. Hector made his way through the long corridors of the castle without seeing another soul. He passed guard stations where steaming mugs sat alone on desk tops, passed open doors to spacious rooms, passed blank view screens. He saw scanning cameras set high up on the corridor wall every few meters, but they seemed to be off. Once or twice he thought he might have heard scuffling and the muffled sounds of men struggling, but he never saw a single person.

Then the big green double doors of the dueling machine chamber came into view. One of them was open, and he could see the machine itself, dimly lit inside.

Still no one in sight!

Hector sprinted into the big, arched-ceiling room and ran straight to the main control desk of the machine. He started setting the power when all the lights in the chamber blazed on blindingly.

From all the doors around the chamber, white-helmeted guards burst in, guns in their hands. A view screen high above flashed into life and a furious man with a bald, bullet-shaped head shouted:

'There he is! Get him!'

Before Hector could move, he felt the flaming pain of a stun bolt smash him against the control desk. As he sank to the floor, consciousness spiraling away from him, he heard Kor ordering:

'Now arrest all the traitors who were helping him. If they resist, kill them!'

Hector's head was buzzing. He couldn't get his eyes open all the way. He seemed to be in a tiny unlit cubicle, metal-walled, with a blank view screen staring at him. Something was on his head, something else strapped around his chest. He couldn't see his hands; they were down on his lap and his head wouldn't move far enough to look at them. Nor would his hands move, despite his will.

He heard voices. Whether they were outside the cubicle or inside his head, he couldn't tell.

'What do you mean, nothing? He must have *some* thoughts in his head!'

'Yes, Minister Kor, there are. But they are so random, so

patternless ... I've never examined a brain like his. I don't see how he can walk straight, let alone think.'

'He is a natural telepath,' Kor's harsh voice countered. 'Perhaps he's hiding his true thought patterns from you.'

'Under the influence of the massive drug doses we've given him? Impossible?'

'The drugs might not affect him.'

'No, that couldn't be. His physical condition shows that the drugs have stupefied him almost completely.'

A new voice piped up. 'The monitor shows that the drugs are wearing off; he's beginning to regain consciousness.'

'Dose him again,' Kor ordered.

'More drugs? Theeffect could be dangerous ... even fatal.'

'Must I repeat myself? The Watchman is a natural telepath. If he regains full consciousness inside the dueling machine, he can disappear at will. The consequences of *that* will be fatal ... to you!'

Hector tried to open his eyes fully, but the lids felt gummy, as though they'd been glued together. *Inside the dueling machine! If I can get myself together before they put me under again* ... His hands weighed two hundred kilos apiece, and he still couldn't move his head. But through his half-open eyes he could see that the view screen was softly glowing, even though blank. The machine was on. *They've been trying to pick my brain,* he realized.

'Here's the syringe, Doctor,' another voice said. 'It's fully loaded.'

Frantically, Hector tried to brush the cobwebs from his mind. *Concentrate on Acquatainia,* he told himself. *Concentrate!* But he could hear the footsteps approaching his booth.

And then his mind seemed to explode. His whole body wrenched violently with a flood of alien thought pouring through him.

*

One moment Odal was sitting in the Acquatainian dueling machine, thinking about Geri Dulaq. An instant later he

191

knew he was in Kerak, and someone else was in the dueling machine with him. Hector! His mind was open and Odal could look deep ... A flash like a supernova explosion rocked Odal's every fiber. Two minds exposed to each other, fully, amplified and cross-linked by the circuits of the machine, fused together inescapably. Every nerve and muscle in both their bodies arched as though a hundred thousand volts of electricity were shooting through them.

Odal! Hector realized. He could see into Odal's mind as if it were his own. In a strange, double-visioned sort of way, he *was* Odal ... himself and Odal, both at the same time. *And Odal, sharing Hector's mind, became Hector.*

Hector saw long files of cadets marching wearily in heavy gray uniforms, felt the weight of the lumpy field packs on their backs, sweated under the scorching sun.

Odal felt the thrill of a boy's first sight of a star ship as it floated magnificently in orbit.

Now Hector was running through the narrow streets of an ancient town, running with a dozen other teenagers in brown uniforms, wielding clubs, shouting in the night shadows, smashing windows on certain shops and homes where a special symbol had been crudely painted only a few minutes earlier. And if anyone came outside to protest, they smashed him, too.

Odal saw a Star Watch instructor sadly shaking his head at his/Hector's attempts to command the bridge of a training ship.

Standing at attention, face frozen in a grim scowl, while the Leader harangued an assembly of a half-million troops and citizens on the anniversary of his ascent to power.

Running after the older boys, trying to get them to let you into the game; but they say you're too small, too dumb, and above all too clumsy.

Holding back the tears of anger and fright while the captain slowly explained why your parents had been taken away. He was almost using baby talk. He didn't like this task, didn't like sending grown-ups to wherever it was that they put bad people. But Mother and Father were bad. They had said bad things about the Leader. And now he would become a soldier and help the Leader and kill all the bad people.

Playing ball in zero gee with four other cadets, floating in the huge, metal-ribbed spheroidal gym, laughing, trying to toss the ball without flipping yourself into a weightless tumble.

Smashing the smug face of the upperclassman who called his parents traitor. His bloody, surprised face. Kneeing, clubbing, kicking him into silence. No one will mention that subject again.

Standing, shaking with exertion and fear, gun in hand, wanting to kill, wanting to please the girl who screamed for death, but looking into the face of the downed man and realizing that nothing, NOTHING, warrants taking a human life.

Clubbing the moon-faced Dulaq, smashing him down into shrieking blood as the six of you hammered him to death, telling yourself he's an enemy, an enemy, if I don't kill him he'll kill me, if I don't kill him the Leader will find someone else who will.

Half-thoughts, emotions, snatches of memory. A mother's face, the special smell of your own room, the sound of laughter. The forgotten past, the buried past, the warmth of the fireplace at home after a day in the snow, the fragrance of Father's pipe, the satisfied purring of the soft-furred kitten in your arms.

Leaving home saying good-bye, Dad still unconvinced that you belonged in the Star Watch. Driving off with the captain, away from the house that was empty now. Fumbling, faltering through training, somehow passing, but always by the barest margin. Being the best, first in the ranks : best student, best athlete, best soldier. Always the best. Learning the real mission of the Star Watch: protect the peace. Learning how to hate, how to kill, and above all, how to revenge yourself against Acquatainia.

Meeting and merging, spiraling together, memories of a lifetime intertwining, interlinking, brain synapses flashing, chemical balances subtly changing, two lives, two histories, two personalities melting together more completely than any two minds had ever known before. Hector and Odal, Odal/Hector – in the flash of that instant when they met in the dueling machine they became briefly one and the same.

And when one of the Kerak meditechs noted the power surging through the machine and turned it off, each of the two young men became an individual again. But a different individual than before. Neither of them could be the same as before. They were linked, irrevocably.

*

'What is it?' Kor snapped. 'What caused the machine to use power like that?'

The meditech shrugged inside his white lab coat. 'The Watchman is in there alone. I don't understand . . .'

Furious, Kor bustled toward Hector's booth. 'If he's recovered and escaped, I'll . . .'

Both doors opened simultaneously. From one booth stepped Hector, clear-eyed, straight-backed, tall and lean and blond. His face was curiously calm, almost smiling. He glanced across to the other booth.

Odal stood there. Just as tall and lean and blond as Hector, with almost exactly the same expression on his face : a knowing expression, a satisfaction that nothing would ever be able to damage.

'You !' Kor shouted. 'You've returned.'

For half an instant they all stood there frozen : Hector and Odal at opposite ends of the dueling machine, Kor stopped in mid-stride about halfway between them, four meditechs at the control panels, a pair of armed guards slightly behind Kor. Kerak's wan bluish sun was throwing a cold early-morning light through the stone-ribbed chamber's only window.

'You are under arrest,' Kor said to Odal. 'And as for you, Watchman, we're not finished with you.'

'Yes you are,' Hector said evenly as he walked slowly and deliberately toward the Intelligence Minister.

Kor frowned. Then he saw Odal advancing toward him too. He took a step backward, then turned to the two guards. 'Stop them ...'

Too late. Like a perfectly synchronized machine, Odal and Hector launched themselves at the guards and knocked them both unconscious before Kor could say another word. Picking up a fallen guard's pistol, Odal pointed it at Kor. Hector retrieved the other gun and covered the cowering meditechs.

'Into the prisoners' cells, all of you,' Odal commanded.

'You'll die for this!' Kor screamed.

Odal jabbed him in the ribs with the pistol. 'Everyone dies sooner or later. Do you want to do it here and now?'

Kor went white. Trembling, he marched out of the chamber and toward the cell block.

There were guards on duty at the cells. One of them Odal recognized as a member of Romis' followers. They locked up the rest, then hurried back upstairs toward Kor's office.

'You take this pistol,' Odal said to the guard as they hurried up a flight of stone steps. 'If we see anyone, tell them you're taking us to be questioned by the Minister.'

The guard nodded. Hector tucked his pistol out of sight inside his cover-alls.

'We've only got a few minutes before someone discovers Kor in the cells,' Odal said to Hector. 'We must reach Romis and get out of here.'

Twice they were stopped by guards along the corridors, but both times were permitted to pass. Kor's outer office was empty; it was still too early for his staff to have shown up.

The guard used Kor's desktop communicator to reach

Romis, his fingers shaking slightly at the thought of exposing himself to the Minister's personal equipment.

Romis' face, still sleepy-looking, took shape on the desk-top view screen. His eyes widened when he recognized Odal.

'What? . . .'

Hector stepped into view. 'I escaped from your ship,' he explained swiftly, 'but got caught by Kor when I tried to get to the dueling machine here. Odal jumped back from Acqua-tainia. We've got Kor locked up temporarily. If you're going to move against Kanus, this is the morning for it. You've only got a few minutes to act.'

Romis blinked. 'You . . . you've locked up Kor? You're at the Intelligence Ministry?'

'Yes,' Odal said. 'If you have any troops you can rely on, get them here immediately. We're going to release as many of Kor's prisoners as we can, but we'll need more troops and weapons to hold this building against Kor's private army. If we can hang on here and get to Kanus, I think most of the army will go over to your side. We can win without blood-shed, perhaps. But we must act quickly!'

*

Sitting on the edge of his bed, staring at the two young blond faces on his bedside view screen, Romis struggled to put his thoughts in order.

'Very well. I'll send every unit I can count on to hold the Intelligence Ministry. Major Odal, perhaps you can contact some of the people you know in the army.'

'Yes,' said Odal. 'Many of their officers are right here, under arrest.'

Romis nodded. 'I'll call Marshal Lugal immediately. I think he'll join us.'

'But we've got to get Kanus before he can bring the main force of the army into action,' Hector said.

'Yes, yes of course. Kanus is at his retreat in the mountains. It's not quite dawn there. Probably he's still asleep.'

'Is there a dueling machine there?' Odal asked.

'I don't know. There might be. I've heard rumors about his having one installed for his own use recently . . .'

'All right,' Hector said. 'Maybe we can jump there.'

'Not until we've freed the prisoners and made certain this building is well defended,' said Odal.

'Right,' Hector agreed.

'There's much to do,' Odal said to the Foreign Minister. 'And not a second to waste.'

'Yes,' Romis agreed.

The tri-di image snapped off, leaving him looking at a dead-gray screen set into the side of his bed table. Romis shook his head, as though trying to clear it of the memory of a dream.

It could be a trap, he told himself. *One of Kor's insidious maneuvers. But the Star Watchman was there; he wouldn't help Kor. Or was it the Watchman? Might it have been an impersonator?*

'Trap or not,' Romis said aloud, 'we'll never have another opportunity like this . . . if it's real.'

He made up his mind. In three minutes he placed three tri-di calls. The deed was done. He was either going to free Kerak of its monster, or kill several hundred good men – including himself.

He got up from bed, dressed swiftly, and called for an air car. Then he opened the bed-table drawer and took out a palm-sized pistol.

His butler appeared at the door. 'Sir, your air car is ready. Will you require a pilot?'

'No,' said Romis, tucking the gun into his belt. 'I'll go alone. If I don't call you by noon, then . . . open the vault behind the bed, read the instructions there, and try to save yourself and the other servants. Good-by.'

Before the stunned butler could say another word, Romis strode past him and out toward the air car.

*

Kanus was abruptly awakened by a terrified servant.

'What is it?' the Leader grumbled, sitting up slowly in the immense circular bed. The sun had barely started to touch the distant snow-capped peaks that were visible through the giant room's floor-to-ceiling windows.

'A . . . a call from the Minister of Intelligence, sir.'

'Don't stand there, put him through!'

The servant touched an ornamented dial next to the doorway. Part of the wall seemed to dissolve into a very grainy, shadowy image of Kor. He appeared to be sitting on a hard bench in a dimly lit, stone-walled cell.

'What's going on?' Kanus demanded. 'Why have you awakened me?'

'It has happened, my Leader,' Kor said quietly, unemotionally. 'The traitors are making their move. I've been locked in one of my own cells . . .'

'What?' Kanus sat rigidly upright in the bed.

Kor smiled. 'The fools think they can win by capturing me and holding the Intelligence Ministry. They overlooked a few details. For one, I have my pocket communicator. I've monitored their calls. Romis is no doubt on his way to your palace, right now, intent on killing you.'

'Romis! And you're locked up!'

Raising his hands in a gesture of calm, Kor went on, 'No need to be overly alarmed, my Leader. They are merely exposing themselves, at last. We can crush them.'

'I'll call out the army,' Kanus said, his voice rising.

'Some parts of the army may turn out to be disloyal to you,' Kor answered. 'Your personal guards should be sufficient, however, to stop these traitors. If you could detach a division or so to recapture the Ministry building, and have your own dueling machine there guarded, that should take care of most of it. Romis is flying into your hands, so it should be a simple matter to deal with him when he arrives.'

'My dueling machine? They're coming through my dueling machine?'

'Only two of them: the traitor Odal, and the Watchman.'

'I'll have them killed by inches!' Kanus roared. 'And Romis, too!'

'Yes, of course. But it will be important to recapture the Intelligence Ministry and free me. And also, you should be ready to deal with any elements of the army and space fleet that refuse to follow your orders.'

'Traitors! Traitors everywhere! I'll have them all killed!'

Kanus banged the control stud over his bed and the wall screen went dark. He began screaming orders to the cringing servant, still standing by the doorway. Within minutes he was robed and hurrying down the hallway toward the room where he had his own private dueling machine.

A squad of guards met him at the door to the dueling machine room.

'Keep that machine off!' Kanus ordered. 'If anyone appears inside the machine, bring him to me at once.'

The guard captain saluted.

Another servant appeared at Kanus' elbow. 'Foreign Minister Romis has arrived, my Leader. He . . .'

'Bring him to my office. At once!'

Kanus strode angrily back to his office. Two guards, armed and helmeted, stood at the door. He brushed past them and stalked inside. Romis was already there, standing by the window alongside the elevated desk.

'Traitor!' Kanus screamed at the sight of the diplomat. 'Assassin! Guards, cut him down!'

Startled, Romis reached for the gun at his waist. But the guards were already inside the office, guns drawn.

Romis hesitated. Then the guards took off their helmets to reveal two blond heads, two lean, grinning faces.

'We arrived at your dueling machine sooner than you thought we would,' Odal said to Kanus. 'It was a simple matter to overpower the guards at the door and take their uniforms.'

'We left when your squad of guards arrived,' Hector added, 'and came here, just a few steps ahead of you.'

Kanus' knees boggled.

Romis relaxed. His hands dropped to his sides. 'It's all over, Chancellor. You are deposed. My men have seized the Intelligence Ministry; most of the army is against you. You can avoid a good deal of bloodshed by surrendering yourself to me and ordering your guards not to fight their countrymen.'

Kanus tried to shriek, but no sounds would come from his throat. Wild-eyed, he threw himself between Odal and Hector and dashed to the door.

'Don't shoot him!' Romis shouted. 'We need him alive if we're going to prevent a civil war!'

*

Kanus raced blindly down the halls to the dueling machine. Without a word to the startled guards standing around the machine, he punched a half-dozen buttons on the control board and bolted into one of the booths. He slapped the neurocontacts to his head and chest and took a deep, long breath. His pounding heart slowed, steadied. His eyes slid shut. His body relaxed.

He was sitting on a golden throne at the head of an enormously long hall. Throngs of people lined the richly tapestried walls, and the most beautiful women in the galaxy sat, bejeweled and leisurely, on the cushioned steps at his feet. At the bottom of the steps knelt Sir Harold Spencer, shackled, blinded, his once proud uniform grimy with blood and filth. No, not blind. Kanus wanted him to see, wanted to look into the Star Watch Commander's eye as he described in great detail how the old man would be slowly, slowly killed.

And now he was floating through space, alone, unprotected from the vacuum and radiation but perfectly comfortable, perfectly at ease. Suns passed by him as he sailed majestically through the galaxy, his galaxy, his personal conquest. He saw a planet below him. It displeased him. He extended a hand toward it. Its cities burst into flames. He could hear the screams of their inhabitants, hear them begging him for mercy. Smiling, he let them roast.

Mountains were chiseled away to become statues of Kanus the Conqueror, Kanus the All-Powerful. Throughout the galaxy men knelt in worship before him.

They feared him. Yet more, they loved him. He was their Leader, and they loved him because he was all-powerful. His word was the law of nature. He could suspend gravity, eclipse stars, bestow life or take it.

He stood before the kneeling multitudes, smiling at some, frowning at those who displeased him. They curled and writhed like leaves in flame. But there was one who was not kneeling. One tall, silver-haired man, straight and slim, walking purposively toward him.

'You must give yourself up,' said Romis gravely.

'Die!' Kanus shouted.

But Romis kept advancing toward him. 'Your guards have surrendered. You've been in the dueling machine for two hours now. Most of the army has refused to obey you. The Kerak Worlds have repudiated you. Kor has commited suicide. There is some fighting going on, however. You can end it by surrendering to me.'

'I am the master of the universe! No one can stand before me!'

'You are sick,' Romis said stiffly. 'You need help.'

'I'll kill you!'

'You cannot kill me. You are helpless . . .'

Everything began to fade, shrink away, dim into darkness. There was nothing now but grayness, and Romis' grave, uncompromising figure standing before him.

'You need help. We will help you.'

Kanus could feel tears filling his eyes. 'I am alone,' he whimpered. 'Alone . . . and afraid.'

His face a mixture of distaste and pity, Romis extended his hand. 'We will help you. Come with me.'

*

Professor Leoh squinted at his wrist screen and saw that it was four minutes before lift-off. The bright red sun of Acquatainia was near zenith. A warm breeze wafted across the spaceport.

'I hope he can get here before we leave,' Geri was saying to Hector. 'We owe him . . . well, something.'

Hector started to nod, then noticed a trim little air car circling overhead. It banked smartly against the cloud-puffed sky and glided to a landing not far from the gleaming shuttle craft that stood before them. Down from its cockpit clambered the lithe figure of Odal.

Hector trotted out to meet him. The two men shook hands, both of them smiling.

'I never realized before,' Leoh said to the girl, 'how much they resemble each other. They look almost like brothers.'

Odal was wearing his light-blue uniform again; Hector was in civilian tunic and shorts.

'I'm sorry to be so late,' Odal said to Geri as he came toward her. 'I wanted to bring you a wedding present, and had to hunt all over Kerak for one of these . . .'

He handed Geri a small plastic box filled with earth. A single, thin bluish leaf had pushed up above the ground.

'It's an eon tree,' Odal explained to them. 'They've become very rare. It will take a century to reach maturity, but once grown it will be taller than any other tree known.'

Geri smiled at him and took the present.

'I wanted to give you a new life,' Odal went on, 'in exchange for the new life you've given me.'

Hector said, 'We wanted to give you something, too. But with the wedding and everything we just haven't had the time to breathe, practically. But we'll send you something from Mars.'

They chatted for a few more minutes, then the loudspeaker summoned Hector and Geri to the ship.

Standing beside Leoh, watching the two of them walk arm in arm toward the ship, Odal asked, 'You're going to return to Carinae?'

'Yes.' Leoh nodded. 'Hector will join me there in a few months, he and Geri. We've got a lifetime of work ahead of us. It's a shame you can't work with us. Now that we know interstellar teleportation is possible, we've got to find out how it works and why. We're going to open up the stars to *real* colonization, at last.'

Looking wistfully at Geri as she rode the lift up to the shuttle's hatch, Odal said, 'I think it would be best for me to stay away from them. Besides, I have my own duties in Kerak. Romis is teaching me the arts of government ... peaceful, law-abiding government, just as you have in the Commonwealth.'

'That's a big job,' Leoh admitted, 'cleaning up after the mess Kanus made.'

'You'd be interested to know that Kanus is being treated psychonically, in the dueling machine. Your invention is being turned into a therapeutic device.'

'So I've heard,' the old man said. 'Its use as a dueling machine is only one possible application for the machine. Look what it did to you and Hector. I never realized that two men could be so dramatically drawn together.'

It was Odal's turn to smile. 'I learned a lot in that moment with Hector in the machine.'

'So did he. And yet,' Leoh's voice took on a hint of regret, 'I almost wish he were the old Hector again. He's so ... so mature now. No more scatterbrain. He doesn't even whistle any more. He'll be a great man in a few years. Perhaps a Star Watch commander someday. He's completely changed.'

As they watched, Hector and Geri waved from the hatch of the shuttle craft. The hatch slid shut, but somehow

Hector's hand got caught still outside. A crewman had to reopen the hatch, glaring at the red-faced Watchman.

Leoh began laughing. 'Well, perhaps not *completely* changed after all,' he said with some relief.

A WRINKLE IN TIME

Madeleine L'Engle

Charles Wallace Murry, who goes searching through 'a wrinkle in time' for his lost father, finds himself on an evil planet where all life is enslaved by a huge pulsating brain known as IT.

How Charles, his sister Meg, and his friend Calvin find and free his father makes this a very special and exciting mixture of fantasy and science fiction, which all the way through is dominated by the funny and mysterious trio of guardian angels known as Mrs Whatsit, Mrs Who, and Mrs Which.

A Newbery Medal winner.

THE OGRE DOWNSTAIRS

Diana Wynne Jones

Caspar and Johnny pelted up to Gwinny's room regardless of noise. Johnny thought she was on fire, Caspar that she was being eaten away by acids. They burst into the room and stood staring. Gwinny did not seem to be there. Her lamp was lit, her bed empty, her window shut, and her dollshouse and other things arranged around as usual, but they could not see Gwinny.

'She's gone,' said Caspar helplessly.

'No, I haven't,' said Gwinny, her voice quivering rather. 'I'm up here.' She appeared to be hanging from the ceiling and looked a bit like a puppet. 'And I can't come down,' she added.

She couldn't either. At least not until the *vol. pulv.* splashed on her from Johnny's chemistry set had worn off ...

SPACE HOSTAGES

Nicholas Fisk

Everything was as usual that summer evening in Little
Mowlesbury, except for one thing – a brilliant star that appeared,
came nearer and nearer, and finally, with a tearing shriek of
blasting jets, landed on the cricket pitch, burning the grass to
a fine grey powder. It was a secret space craft and before anyone
could protest the man inside had kidnapped the first children
who came flocking to see it and lifted the ship far into the sky
again. And then they discovered that he was dying and they had
to find out how to work the ship!

THE GUARDIANS

John Christopher

It is the future, and mankind is at peace. The working week has
been halved, and all men think alike – or that's the idea. But
life has become difficult for Rob in the State Boarding School to
which he was consigned on his father's death, so he crosses the
terrifying no-man's-land into the country, alone and afraid.
There, unbelievably he finds friends to help him construct a new
identity and is settling into a happy, harmonious life when he
discovers the terrifying inhuman way in which all this delightful
tranquillity is imposed . . .

This serious, frightening and sharply convincing book is by an
author who is already deservedly well known for his stories of
the future. It won the Guardian Award for 1971.

For readers of eleven and over.

If you have enjoyed reading this book and would like to know about others which we publish, why not join the Puffin Club? You will be sent the club magazine, *Puffin Post*, four times a year and a smart badge and membership book. You will also be able to enter all the competitions. For details of cost and an application form, send a stamped addressed envelope to:

The Puffin Club Dept A
Penguin Books Limited
Bath Road
Harmondsworth
Middlesex